THE JESUS ULTIMATUM

To Skate + Fingers

Much Love,
Merry Jeremy

THE JESUS ULTIMATUM

GERARD BROOKER

TATE PUBLISHING & *Enterprises*

Published by Tate Publishing & Enterprises, LLC
127 E. Trade Center Terrace | Mustang, Oklahoma 73064 USA
1.888.361.9473 | www.tatepublishing.com

Tate Publishing is committed to excellence in the publishing industry. The company reflects the philosophy established by the founders, based on Psalm 68:11,
"The Lord gave the word and great was the company of those who published it."

Published in the United States of America

ISBN: 978-1-61566-120-6
1. Fiction, Christian, General
2. Fiction, Religious
10.01.20

ACKNOWLEDGEMENTS

A God who allows me to question
and to rage against the way it is.

Donna Della Valle for helping me with the title.
The Bethel, CT post office personnel for their
advice about being a post mail worker.

Sue Blackmore for sharing the
story of her Jimmy with me.

The great teachers who have encouraged
me to question everything they taught me.

Frank Johnston (retired Captain, FDNY) for
helping me understand how a fire department works.

Ken Stefanak (retired, FDNY) for conveying
to me what it means to be a firefighter.

Christy V. Doyle for her technical assistance.

Justin O'Connell, a friend, for lending
to me his wisdom about a loving God.

Again, to the God of my heart, if I
seek to know too much it is only because I
would have prayed all night with you.

And to the staff at Tate Publishing, especially
Kalyn McAlister, whose editing skills have made this
book whole, Leah LeFlore for a wonderful cover,
and Stefanie Rooney for a great interior design.

I am grateful to you all for your gifts to me.

to his ex. "Look at his big car," he'd say. Or, "He even has a cook who probably makes his bed."

It didn't take him long to convince Ellen. The children were happy that they didn't have to go there on Sunday mornings anymore.

Actually, they were an embarrassment half the time in church, pulling out rolls of toilet paper from their pockets to wipe their noses, doing little butterfly farts before laughing at the grownups in the next row back. The two boys learned how to maximize the effect by waiting to do the deed until everyone was kneeling.

After a while of weird kids and a wife he wasn't crazy about, he began to drink more beer and get more quiet. Delivering mail on foot for eight hours a day was his excuse for wanting to be alone. He'd go to the movies by himself, or maybe have a beer in a bar once in a while, though that was not one of his favorite things to do. Sitting on park benches and watching the pigeons strut their stuff was a favorite. Cocky little birds begging for peanuts while walking around like they owned the joint. He liked to watch them lunge for the imaginary peanuts that he pretended to throw on the ground.

It was getting so that after a while he just didn't know who he was anymore. He stopped doing things. Not that he used to be the world's most active guy. But he began to stop doing the little things. Like watching TV with the wife and kids. Even quit the mailman's bowling league. You think that might draw a few questions from the guys on the job. It didn't, probably because he was never one of the guys. He was there, but never had the give 'n take.

PROLOGUE

He had a nice relationship with God. You know, talked to him during the day, mostly when delivering the mail. Lately, though, the conversation—if you can call it that—has been more frequent, probably because things were happening in his life. Mainly, his divorce. He even let on to Jesus one day that if he ever wanted to talk to him, for any reason, that it would be okay with him. At first, Francis thought it was plain stupid to speak to him that way. On the other hand, he was mostly okay with it because down deep, he meant it humbly. Asking God to show up came from a longing he had for a personal God. He just didn't want him showing up in the apartment without notice. "God, if I ever come back into the living room after getting a beer and you're sitting in my blue chair, I'll drop dead from fright. So please don't do that."

There's a difference between being afraid and scared, he reasoned.

He was not a religious man. Hardly. He used to be. But when he and his family got singled out for coming to church late, and then for the kids' dirty sneakers, well, something kind of snapped. Actually, he hardly had enough money to keep himself in beer. His life sucked, and he went to church to kind of feel better, and that didn't happen.

He was looking for an excuse to quit. Church, that is. So, he started to point out things about the pastor

DEDICATION

To Lt. James W. Blackmore and Captain Scott La Piedra, FDNY, who died side by side in the summer of 1998 fighting a fire in Brooklyn. "No greater love has any man than this, that he lay down his life for his friends." How much greater is it that they did it for strangers.

To the firefighters of Engine Company 332 and Ladder Company 176, Brooklyn, NY.

I hold each of you, past and present, in awe, and this is how it should be.

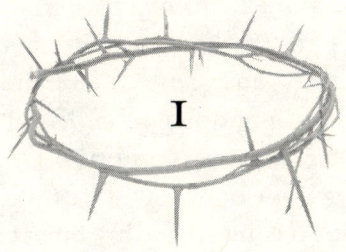

I

About the same time that Jesus came to see him, he and Ellen got divorced. It wasn't bad, except for the kids. You know, how they get so disappointed, so mad at you. They stayed with his wife, who got a job at the dry cleaners across the street, and he moved down the block. He liked the old neighborhood. Astoria, Queens, to be exact. He got himself a dingy little studio apartment on Grand Avenue and 32nd Street. The kids stayed up near Steinway Street, the old rental, in a large apartment house. It was better for them to stay there, he thought. They could stay in the same school, keep their friends, and be with their mother. The judge was a good guy, and Ellen settled for child support; a good thing for Francis, because he didn't figure anyone would ever marry her again. This way, at least, the payments would end someday, even though he'd be broke for the next dozen years or so.

He was not a religious man. He liked to think that he was a spiritual man, although he was not sure what that meant. It might have just been something to soothe his guilt for not going to church anymore. All that nun's stuff in grammar school, you know, made him a guilty person, a very guilty person for practically just taking a breath. How if he didn't go to Mass every Sunday, he'd commit the big one and be doomed to hell. Unless he got rid of it by telling it to a priest on Saturday. And if he ate meat on Friday, well, hell would be his lot. It just didn't make sense to him to watch his father put the burgers in the frying pan at 11:50 p.m. and start the burner five minutes later so they'd be ready a minute after midnight. He'd think, *If these clocks are fast, I'm doomed.*

He was scared that he would break the Sacred Heart of Jesus by masturbating, which he did a lot when he was a kid. The Sacred Heart story they told him was all so gooey to him that after a while he didn't even want to think of it any more. Blood flowing from his heart when he still wasn't even dead. You could see the heart in the statues, which his mother had one of in the hallway leading to his bedroom. Every time he passed that statue, he got the willies when he'd see the cutaway heart.

It didn't help when the nuns told him that he'd go to fire if he even thought what they called "bad thoughts." Sister Miriam sat behind the desk one day, closed her eyes, and said, "Now, children, if I even think of a nude man in my thoughts, I'll go to hell." Those weren't the same images that kept rolling around in his head, but he got the point. He was doomed! There was nothing he could do about it.

It got worse when he went to high school, a Catholic high school. It seemed like the more educated he got, the less he believed this stuff. He became a smart aleck kid and got ass whipped so many times by his religious teachers that even sometimes today when he thinks about it he can't even sit down. He didn't know it at the time, but the drift away from religion was beginning. It just didn't make any sense to him that God could ever want to punish anyone.

He began to enter into what he called a "deep conversation" with God. He had lots of time on his hands. He worked an eight-hour day delivering the mail by foot, which he wanted. He even delivered his own incoming mail. He always thought that the guys who delivered by trucks were wusses, sissies who couldn't take the cold and the dogs. He figured he'd stay in shape if he did the job on foot. When he got divorced, he really thought walking the mail was a good thing. He could meet chicks.

It didn't work out that way. He was too shy to just talk with a woman without being introduced. So there he was: divorced, moving into a new place, lots of time on his hands, a loner, dumping his religion, and missing his kids. But just a little bit. Mostly, though, he enjoyed being alone.

Until the day he got a letter from Jesus.

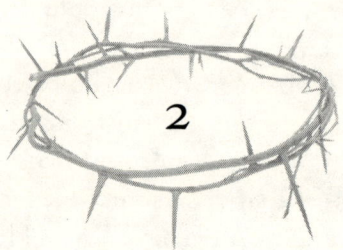

2

Dear Francis,

I heard you when you told me how scared you would be if I just showed up in your living room. So, I decided to write a letter to you before I come to your apartment. That is, if you agree to see me alone.

You're probably wondering if this is a joke by one of your friends at the post office. Let me assure you, this is not a joke. If you look at the postage stamp on this envelope, you'll see that it is in honor of U.S. coal miners. It is a stamp that I had made up myself here in heaven. As you might know, there isn't now, nor has there ever been, a stamp in honor of coal miners. As an aside, let me say I don't know why not, as no one deserves it more. But that is, for now, neither here nor there.

I have chosen you because you are a sincere man who is trying to believe in me. I know it is hard for you to believe in me. Your parents should have called you Thomas instead of Francis. You're one of those humans who live in their heads, who believe only when they can put their hands on the proof.

I've got a proposition for you. I want you to help me out with something. First, though, I want to tell you ahead of time that at seven o'clock next Monday night I'll be at your apartment, sitting in your favorite chair, the blue one you sit in to watch TV. If you are not by yourself, I will not come.

With warm regards,
Jesus Christ

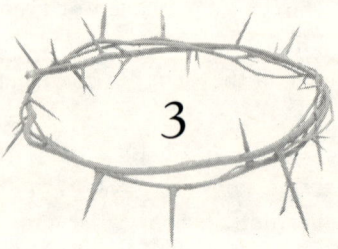

3

He received the letter in the Wednesday mail. He didn't open it until about eight o'clock that night, which was his custom. He didn't know why, but he always got a kick out of delivering mail to himself. Putting his own mail into his little mailbox made him feel like someone knew he existed. His kids were mad at him and his ex didn't speak to him; so even though most of the mail was court stuff, bills, or junk, it was good to know that someone knew he was alive. He hardly ever got a real letter. Once in a while a card from Uncle Jimmy or Aunt Priscilla. But that was it. At least for now. Maybe when he got his act straight and had a few friends, he'd get more letters, personal stuff.

At first, he didn't take the letter from Jesus too seriously. Who would take a letter signed Jesus Christ seriously? He figured he'd just say nothing and wait a few days until the joker revealed himself before exploding. Nothing happened on Thursday, nothing on Friday. He checked his mail very carefully on Saturday, Joe's day to deliver, to see if a new letter was there. He guessed that there'd be a follow-up by the prankster. Nothing.

He was getting a bit anxious by the end of the day on Sunday. He was beginning to sweat and take it sort of seriously. It really didn't make him too nervous that the Son of God might be in contact. Even though he wasn't religious anymore, he always had a kind of true feeling in his gut that if God ever wanted to show up in his life, he'd welcome him, really welcome him. He just didn't like to talk about this kind of stuff with anyone. He was afraid to actually see him. If he could write letters back and forth and he'd just tell him what to do, it wouldn't be a problem. But to actually look at God, well, that's something else, something entirely else.

His anxiety led him to do something rash. "Father Bill, this is Francis. Francis, the mailman. My wife and I used to go to your church. I hope you remember me. I'd like to stop by and talk to you about something that has come up in my life recently, something I've got to tell someone. I don't know how to handle it."

Francis thanked him for seeing him. He knew from the way he looked at him that he remembered him. "You're the guy who always came late and whose kids used my church for all kinds of bathroom shenanigans. Am I right?"

Just cutting past all his crap is the best way for me here, he thought.

"Yes, Father, those are the ones."

Satisfied, he asked, "What do you want?"

"I got a letter in the mail a few days ago from, well, let me just say it was signed *Jesus*." The priest stared at him. "Well, yes," he said. He kept on staring.

"Aren't you the lucky one. Getting a letter from God, you say?"

"It was signed by Jesus is what I said. At first, I thought it was a joke and whoever did it would let me know when they couldn't take it any more, I mean, couldn't take it anymore not knowing if I thought it was serious. But no one has said anything. I'm beginning to think the letter might be real."

"Let's see now," he answered, "if I've got this straight. You received a letter a few days ago signed 'Jesus,' and now you're beginning to think it really is Jesus." After a timely pause, he continued. "Now why would he write to you? I mean, he could pick from anyone on the face of this earth. He could pick a holy person, or a man of the cloth. So why would he pick you?"

"I don't really know why. And, frankly, I wish he would have picked you. I mean if this is real."

"Son," he said, "you're a lucky fellow, chosen by God. Right up there now with the fishermen, with Joseph, Moses, and the rest. Why don't you just leave here and get about doing God's business. I'm finding your holiness unbearable." He then told Francis that he had a dinner invitation at a poor widow's house and ushered him out.

There was nowhere else to go. He'd just sort of hold his breath until that night at seven and see what happened. One thing was for sure: He'd have to miss the *Seinfeld* re-runs.

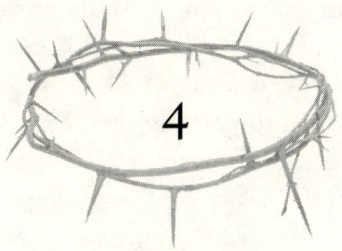

4

He didn't know what to compare his nervousness to that day. Maybe waiting for the lab results on a stomach tumor, or waiting to hear if your child has a chance after the car accident. He didn't know. In some ways, it's even worse waiting to see if God shows up in your living room.

He remembered that the day seemed long. His delivery route was north on the western side of Grand Avenue, from the El at 31st Street to Steinway Street. After the divorce, he was always somewhere between excitement and dread of bumping into his kids or ex on the streets, depending on how things were going between them. If there was a nice word or two from her, he'd like it when he saw any of them between visitation rights. If his payments were late because of a screw-up at the post office and she called to complain, then he didn't like seeing them. He didn't want to see any of them on that day because he was so nervous.

"Hi, Dad!" It was Thomas, his eleven-year-old. "Mom says that I can watch the Yankee game tonight." Whenever he said something like that to his father, it broke his heart a little because one of the nice things between them was watching Yankee games.

Francis gave him a hug, not too tight. They weren't that type of family.

"How's it going, Thomas? The Yankee game, eh. Who's going for them tonight?"

"I don't know," he said before skipping away. "I told my friend I'd help him deliver papers. Got to go. See you, Dad."

It sounds awful, running off like that. It wasn't. They bumped into each other often enough so that chance meetings lost their significance after a while, even though every time he'd see one of his sons accidentally he wasn't the same for an hour or two. Knowing that he wouldn't be seeing him that night made him feel ashamed of himself, such a failure that he couldn't even stay in a marriage to bring up the kids.

He finished about five each night, give or take fifteen minutes, depending. He started to think whether he should get something special for seven o'clock. There was no telling what Jesus liked or even if he eats. Or drinks, for that matter. So, he decided to stop at the deli and get some orange juice, figuring that would be healthy and sunshiny, all good stuff.

"Jesus, would you like a glass of orange juice?" he practiced.

He decided not to go to the apartment. It gave him the willies to think that Jesus could show up right at seven o'clock, on the dot. Probably would. He thought, when God says seven o'clock, he probably means seven o'clock, not five after. Besides, he didn't know if he should sit down near the blue chair and wait, or just pretend that he was cool and go about his business.

He decided to go to the Astoria Bar and Grill on 32nd and Grand, right under his rental. He figured that he better not have any beer, as he might get drunk given the circumstances, and that would be very disrespectful.

"Pat, just give me a coke with a twist of lemon." Now, the AB and G wasn't exactly a twist of lemon kind of place.

"You'll get a coke and that's all." He looked at the mailman kind of funny. "So you don't like the beer here anymore?"

"It's not that. It's just that I need to have a clear head on tonight." Pat gave him a knowing smile, and thankfully, let it go. In and around checking his watch about every minute, Francis had two more cokes. At five to seven, he got more nervous and confused. Was it better to be a minute early or a minute late for God? Everything he had learned in school said a minute early.

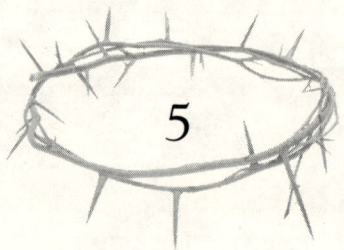

5

This is a terrible moment, he thought. Not terrible in the sense that seeing Jesus is a terrible thing. Not that way. But when he started to walk up the flight of stairs, he was terrified. Just plain scared.

He must have seen a thousand pictures in his life of Jesus, and he suddenly realized that he'd been picturing the Hollywood Jesus since he got the letter. But what if it's God, the Father God, with the beard and all? That would be overwhelming, especially given the way he was. He couldn't even sit on the subway and not notice the way a guy or a woman fixes their hair or the clothes they wear.

Everything started to hit him at once. He tried to stop thinking about all the little things, but couldn't. Where does he get his robes? Does he get his robes, or are they just there? He wondered if he'd be wearing sandals and what they'd be made of. Maybe you don't even have to worry about those things in heaven. He even began to think about underwear.

Enough, he screamed at himself. *Enough. Now just open the door and see what happens. Stop being a godda ... Stop being a sissy boy!*

He opened the door and flipped on the light switch with his left hand, the way he'd always done it, but this time he was so aware of what he was doing that he felt like a kid tying his shoelaces by himself for the first time.

There he was, sitting in the blue chair. Straight up, like he was very aware of good posture. "Good evening, Francis." He almost fainted. "I know this might be some kind of shock to you, seeing me sitting right here, but I did try to warn you with my letter. I listen, so I knew you might be scared if I just showed up."

What do you say to God when he is sort of apologizing to you?

"Thank you, God," he said.

"It's good to be here with you, Francis. But I'd like to get something straight right away. You see, I'm not God. Well, technically I am, but in practice I'm not. God is my father. It's complicated. Maybe later. Right now I'd like to talk about you."

You've got to know that by now that Francis is almost giddy. Jesus wanting to talk about him. Francis was staring at him with his mouth open.

"Do I call you God or Jesus?" he asked.

"You can call me Jesus, but just to simplify things. I'm actually also God."

Francis knew that Jesus could tell what he was

going through. *Well, yeah, duhh, I guess he can.* "Maybe you'd rather gather yourself together first, take care of business, put the groceries away."

He closed the door. "Do you mind if I sit down?" he asked.

"Hey, it's your house," he responded in a soft voice.

For some reason, this triggered all the cynicism that had been growing in him for a long time to burst out of his mouth. "How do I know you're God?"

He seemed amused. "I guess I'll just show you." Suddenly, the lights in the apartment started to blink on and off, on and off, about a million times a second. It was impressive.

"Jesus, I have to tell you that I'm a cynic."

"You don't say," he said.

"What just happened could be some kind of a trick. Maybe you've got a clicker, an electrical clicker that you can just click the juice on and off, like that," he said, snapping his fingers in a nervous habit.

Jesus grinned at Francis who sensed that all was not well, that Jesus was tired of him already. "No, Francis, it's not a trick. I'll just have to reach beyond your skepticism and bump it up a notch. I don't like to do that, because it will be a setback for the very reason I am here." He paused, then said, "Here goes."

All of a sudden, Francis was in this incredibly eerie and enchanting place, as if he was under a spell. Like a kind of high. Not a druggie high, but the way he felt when everything was going right, no worries or problems, when he was getting what he wanted and not thinking about tomorrow. There was a fuzzy charm about it all, a kind of enchantment. He was more than just seeing it. He felt as if he was smelling through his eyes, and touching through his eyes, and hearing through his eyes. He swore, it was like he was tasting it through his eyes.

Then it got really weird, because everything was mixed up. A delicious smell was coming to Francis whenever he touched something. But he didn't know what he was touching. And when he smelled, he was touched gently, but not in his nose, but all over. It was too much for him, so he decided to stay still, to just accept whatever might happen next.

What happened next was that he was back in the apartment with Jesus. He thought he was convinced, but he wasn't sure. Maybe it was a trick, maybe he can cast a spell, or maybe he had sprayed some LSD in the air. He did notice when he came in that the apartment smelled nicer than usual.

Francis thought he'd ask him what he thought of the show, but Jesus just moved on like nothing had happened.

"Jesus, would you like a glass of orange juice?" It was the only thing he could think of.

"Yes, I would," he answered.

He took the container out of the bag. It was warm by now. "I'm afraid it's a little warm. And I don't have ice cubes. It's a tiny fridge. I'm sorry."

"No problem," he said. "I used to drink it warm." So, he gave him a glass, a small glass of the warm juice. "Thank you," he said.

Do you know how weird that is? Francis thought. For Jesus to be saying "thank you" to him?

"I'm going to sit down."

"Francis," he said it like a declaration, "the orange juice is good."

Knowing that the prelims were coming to an end, he began to get very nervous.

"I came here for a reason, and I chose you for a reason," he said.

He thought maybe he should say something like "I am honored, Lord," or "I do not deserve this, Jesus." But he thought that Jesus would just toss it off if he spoke to him like that. He wasn't formal. So, he said what came from his heart. "Thank you."

"I've never been very impressed with those who speak to me with what I call formulas," Jesus said. "I mean, the *Thee* and *Thou* way of talking. I know that a certain amount of it is necessary, especially when large groups are gathered in my name. It's a formality. But, I don't like it much in private conversations.

"I always like it when you talked to me in a natural way. You speak from the heart. And you mean what you say."

He wanted to explain to him that it only seemed that way, that he really didn't know any other way to say it. He wanted to tell Jesus that he'd never been to college, but he figured he probably knew that already. What he blurted out was, "Oh my God, you really listen to us?"

He didn't mean it the way it might have sounded.

"Of course I listen to you. I listen to everyone who

wants to talk with me, even when they do it in the strangest ways. I mean through alcohol, drugs, and sex. I know that they're trying to find something that makes it all seem good and worthwhile. I try to put ideas into the hearts and minds of these folks because I know that they're seeking but don't know how to find. It's the ones who try to find me through power who are the hardest to reach. It's really worse than drugs. Lots of these folks won't let me in one little bit, cut me off."

Francis didn't know where he got the spark from, but he just had to ask him a question. "Why do you let them do it? I mean, why don't you just step in and stop the cr … , I mean, stop the ones who do this?"

"I didn't come here to talk about me, so let's let that go for another time. I want to talk with you. Not because you're the holiest guy here, but because you always mean what you say to me.

"Do you remember the trip you took to Jerusalem when you were a young man?" he asked. Francis wasn't sure if the question was rhetorical or not. He was thinking, *I can't believe I'm trying to figure out if God wants me to answer his question or not. I mean me. Not someone else. Me trying to figure out how to respond to God.* He was about knocked out. So, he stopped the conversation.

"Jesus, I'm sorry, but I think maybe you're here with me under false pretenses. That's right. It's perfect. I mean *pretenses* is perfect. I am the pretender. You see, I don't always mean what I say. I pretend to say the truth. Do you know how many times I've lied to my ex-wife, how many times I've told the kids I'd take them somewhere and didn't show up, or changed my mind, or had too many beers?"

"I know. It's why I said you're not the holiest guy in town. And I said that you always mean what you say to *me,* not necessarily to everyone else."

"You're right. I remember the trip. It was fifteen years ago. And then I got married. It's the only trip I ever took."

"You were walking on the street in Jerusalem where I carried the cross. You got kind of choked up and told me that you would have helped me carry that cross. I remember your words: *I'd have carried that cross for you, Jesus. I'd have carried it until I died.*"

Francis started to feel a bit at ease. "Can I get you some more orange juice?"

"Not right now."

"I could send for some Chinese, if you're hungry." As soon as he said that, the whole thing began to get surreal again. Chinese for Jesus!

"You know, I do like Chinese. And I'm hungry. So, yes, let's get some Chinese."

Perplexed, he asked, "How can you be hungry? You're God."

"Whenever I visit one of the planets, I allow myself to become like you, at least for the time being. It's good for me. Helps me not to forget. Helps me to remember what it's like. Not easy."

"Oh," he muttered. "Is there a special dish you like?"

"How about sweet and sour?"

He got up to make the call when Jesus said, "Sit

down, Francis. I took care of it for you. Let's get back to Jerusalem. When you said you'd help with the cross, I knew you meant it. It made me feel happy when you said that. I wish that you had been around when it happened. I got a little help from a man named Simon, but they kind of forced him to do it."

He seemed to pause and think about his words, which surprised Francis—that he had to think about what he was going to say.

"It's not that I wasn't grateful. It's just that it works better when someone wants to do a thing, instead of being told to do it. But you, you have a generous attitude toward me. I really do believe that you would have carried it till you died."

"I would have," he responded.

"I wasn't surprised you told me that. Ever since you were a little boy, I continually offered gifts to you, and you kept on saying yes. You build up a way of doing things. It's why the heavenly council picked you."

"I don't understand. You offered gifts?"

"Well, not material ones, of course, but spiritual ones. Do you remember the day you had the bully pinned down, and you wanted to bust his face in? At that very instant, I offered you the grace to stop. And you resisted smacking him. Do you remember?"

"Yes, I do. Funny thing; for years I felt like a coward for not busting him."

"And do you remember when you were a precocious twelve-year-old, and the girl next door wanted you to have sex with her. How you both took off your clothes and you stopped?"

"Yeah … excuse me. Yes, I remember. I ran home nearly half undressed."

Just as he was about to speak, the doorbell rang. Sweet and sour for Jesus. He had ordered barbecued spare ribs for them both. Francis began to ask himself how he knew they were his favorite, but then he remembered. The conversation was that good.

Francis put out plates, napkins, and stuff they needed, and two small glasses of juice. They sat down. He waited for Jesus to say grace. There was an awkward silence. It was an entrancing moment for Francis. *My God,* he thought, *I'm really something, a religious star waiting to happen. Jesus picked me to visit. Me.*

For a long time they ate in silence. Jesus spoke first. "Francis, there are a few people you deliver mail to, and I'm here to offer gifts to them. I've tried before, in my own subtle way, but they always manage to say no. I need your help."

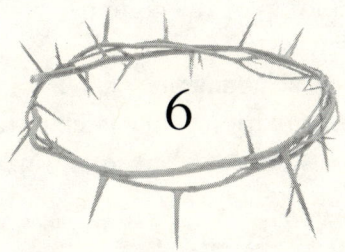

6

He remembered looking at the kitchen clock on the wall. It said 8:35 when Jesus began.

"Tina Remsen lives in the big apartment house at 2609 Steinway Street. She's in unit twenty-nine. She's been married for about fifteen years and is a practicing Methodist, really believes in the Bible. She's a good lady, good mother. She's on hard times now because she doesn't think that she loves her husband any more. He's kind of a jerk, if I must say so myself, who doesn't pay much attention to her. He's become a bit more in love with beer and TV over the past few years than with her.

"My four friends who wrote the wonderful chapters of my life left out an interesting and critical part. They told me later that they thought it wasn't good for the people to know this, that it might take away from my holiness, maybe confuse my followers and hinder the founding of the church.

"I wish they had included it. You see, I fell in love. Not with Mary Magdalene, which some have said, without any imagination. They latch onto her because she showed me kindness. But lots of women showed me kindness.

"I fell in love with Mary Magdalene's friend, whose name is Rachel. Her name means *lamb* in Hebrew. My lamb, with the innocence of purity. We married in a quiet ceremony. Just a plain wedding, no turning water into wine.

"I loved her greatly. You'll never know the pleasure that was mine to know that I loved her. It was a sense of things I never had before I came into the world, something I didn't know in heaven, not in this way. Do you know how being on this earth, how being human for a while was such a rich blessing for me? One that allowed me to know love the way you do? It is full of wonder. It makes me sad when I see people missing the wonder of the gift. Marrying Rachel was a way for me to know in my humanity the power of my love for the Church and for the New Covenant.

"Yes, I loved her greatly. I love her now, at this moment."

Then he said, "You might grow tired, Francis, of hearing me talk about Nazareth. Of all the places my father sent me, Jerusalem, Capernaum, the Galilee, anywhere; my favorite always was Nazareth. It was so right. It was good to walk its roads, dust on my robes, pebbles in my sandals. It was the stuff of the earth.

He stopped, and he seemed like he was about to cry. Francis wanted to ask him more, but he didn't dare. He seemed so human.

"Something terrible might happen to Tina's boy. This is where you come in. I will be mailing a letter to her about what might happen. It will be your job to make sure she gets the letters as well as to speak with her about me, to tell her that I am real and that the letters and what I say in them are real."

Oh, man, Francis thought. "Jesus, how will I know the letters are from you?"

"I told you before. There will be a special postage stamp on the letters, a stamp to honor American coal miners. This is the sign you will know."

He suddenly got different. A palpable seriousness came over him.

"What I am seeing more and more of, Francis, is a lack of faith. Especially here in America, sad to say. It's hard for someone who has many things to think about and guard to believe in things that he cannot see. The Heavenly Council tells me that church attendance has fallen off. That's not so important to me, given the mess that churches have made. If I thought when I walked along the streets of Nazareth, talking with friends and foes about how to love one another, that my words would get organized into a thousand prescriptions iterated from gilded houses of worship, I might have been tempted to do it differently. But in the end, the Father, the Holy Spirit, and I always respect free will.

"You've mentioned a heavenly council. Please tell me what that is."

He leaned over to take one of the barbecued ribs. Francis saw that his fingers were getting sticky, so he went to the sink and wet a small towel with warm water for him. His eyes warmed with a wordless thank you as he took the proffered towel and began answering his question.

"When I came down to be crucified, I was both human and God. I know that's probably a hard thing to grasp. When I was here, I was a human being, the son of Mary and Joseph. I was Jesus of Nazareth like you're Francis of New York. But I agreed with my Father to let the fact that I'm God stay in the background, in my spirit. I was still God, but we agreed to put my powers, for the most part, in a quiet state. We thought that was necessary so I could feel the pain of winning back the possibility for humans to love again. If my powers were too active, I would simply adjust problems to accommodate myself.

"To this day, though, I have kept my human qualities, something most people don't realize. It wasn't like I died and then gave up that I was a person. I'm still a person. A different kind of person, for certain. I'm God. But I still have the potential to feel the same things that you do, even when I'm in heaven."

Francis was getting dizzy. He didn't seem to know who he was anymore. He kept trying to accept that he was Francis T. Meeks, a thirty-eight-year old mailman, a middle-class divorcee with two kids and no interests besides drinking beer and watching TV.

He was just an ordinary guy, less than ordinary, not up to anything in life. But there he was, listening to Jesus Christ, Son of God, explaining to him how he's both divine and human at the same time. He was not even making a big deal out of it. He was just telling him like you'd tell someone that sometimes you have mood swings.

"I know that you're feeling a bit weird about this," Jesus said. "I can tell, my sitting here talking with you. It's not an everyday experience, I know. Try to relax. I promise that I won't do anything that will freak you out. And you can be free to ask me any questions. You can talk as long as you'd like. I've suspended time for now, so you don't have to worry about getting up for work tomorrow."

This made Francis feel better; especially the part about not doing anything different that might make him crazy. He decided to repeat his question again— Jesus wouldn't get offended. Maybe he had meant to answer the first time, but was sidetracked. "Please tell me about the council you have."

"Before I say anything, I want you to know that when our mission is over, here in your neighborhood, that anything I don't want you to remember will just disappear from your mind.

"Now, let me tell you about the Heavenly Council. It's important for me to always remember what it is like here. You're probably thinking that since I am God then, of course, I'll remember. I can do that if I want, but I'd rather not. I'd rather have a really great relationship with some outstanding human beings who know what is going on. That is why I formed the Council.

"It's a group of people who have already died to the earth, people I admire for the way they lived here. They have been sincere people and, of course, continue to be so in heaven. Unlike you, they also accomplished much when they were living here. What you do have in common with them is that you are never deceitful to me. I like that in a person. I really like it when anyone resonates to the spark of goodness.

"I update the council every so often. Things change. Right now, there are mostly old-timers, ready for some relief. There's Albert Schweitzer, Dag Hammarskjold, Arland Williams, Jr., Princess Diana, a man named Juan Ramirez, and a fireman named Jimmy Blackmore—a family guy, the kind of man the Father finds hard to resist. It's a really good group. They picked you for this mission we're on. Each one of them really liked you, and for different reasons. You especially got a big lift from Princess Diana. She likes that you're a good guy, a mensch.

"You'd like them, Francis. I only meet with them when I want to, which is good because they all have regular jobs in heaven. Albert works with the animals, feeding, petting, that kind of thing. Diana with the children who were killed in the Holocaust. And Arland, what a great guy. Wherever I ask him to go, he just keeps on giving of himself, no matter what. Dag I send everywhere to whisper into the ears of diplomats. He tells me that they hardly ever listen."

"What about Juan Ramirez?" Francis asked.

"Juan is the greatest. I don't want anyone to think I have favorites, but I can't help it. Part of being human, I guess, but I really like Mexicans. They're more generous than others, sweeter. They have a leg up on the rest of you. They seem to be born that way. It's hard to get them angry at me, much harder than for most. So, I asked Juan to be on the Council. I want his point of view."

"You said something about a fireman?"

"Yes, that's Jimmy, Jimmy Blackmore. He was killed in a fire in Brooklyn, right across the river there. He was trying to rescue a woman who, in the end, was not even in the burning building. The roof fell down on him. Killed Jimmy and another great fireman named Scott LaPiedra. Since they arrived here over ten years ago, they have been tending to the needs of children who died young, the ones whose fathers are not yet here with them.

"Jimmy always had a special love for children on earth and asked for the assignment here to care for children while they await the day when they will be reunited with their loved ones."

They talked what seemed to be hours about this council. Jesus said that he doesn't meet with them a lot, but really enjoys it when he does. Finds them fascinating, he said. Now and then, he told Francis, he or the Father calls a meeting just because he wants to see them. He tried to tell them that once, but they didn't have much to talk about without there being a serious matter at hand. So, he would just choose any one of a hundred problems on earth, and then ask them how they felt about it.

It was more of a way to keep in touch as a person than it was to intervene and clear up the problem he chose for the agenda. He told Francis that it wasn't the way that his Father wanted to handle things on the earth. Originally, the Father made all the creatures on the earth good, kind, generous, and loving; a lot like Juan.

"Francis, my Father has other, bigger ideas for the creatures he has allowed to be born on this planet. He wanted the most important part of everyone's existence to be about love. He wanted love to be the fulfillment of each person's existence. But then when Adam failed to obey, man's inner spirit seemed to dry up. He started to get stingy and mean. Loving became indifference. There was so much evil around that it seemed like it became a living thing.

"I'll try to explain this a bit. My Father, at some point a long time ago, was disappointed with another planet that had gone bad. The planet does not have a name or even a history. It was recording its own stories at some point, but when things went bad, everything was destroyed.

"You'll never believe how loving it was for him to make me a flesh and blood creature to send to the earth to redeem it. My Father is so in love with humans that he decided to have an indwelling with himself. It was me. He asked me if I would be willing to come down here and try to give the message of love. I even knew what was going to happen to me. I also knew when it would happen.

"If you knew my Father, you'd know why I said yes. He's all about love." He stopped when he saw Francis looking very confused, even overwhelmed.

7

Francis had always suffered from anxiety. With these revelations from Jesus, he began to feel butterflies in his stomach, very active butterflies. He wanted to keep composed.

"Jesus," he asked, "do you mind if I take a Xanax? I take it because sometimes I get so anxious that I think I'll explode. When I get like that, I need something to calm me down."

"Hey, whatever works," he said.

He practically ran into his bedroom to get one. He chewed it before washing it down with an almost-hot glass of water. Then he looked in the mirror, half expecting that he had changed, that maybe there was a glow coming from him. Not that he did anything to merit that, but Jesus was in the next room, and maybe, just maybe.

"Thank you for waiting," he apologized when he returned.

"No problem," he answered before telling Francis about another of the people who refused the gifts he had offered to them.

"This man's name is Richard Darby. His friends call him Dick, probably because he is rather self-centered and boring. I prefer to call him Richard, the name given to him by his mother.

"Richard has a child who's about eleven. She's a bright girl and a loner, probably because her mother was killed in a car accident about two years ago. Her dad was driving the car and he was very careless. He deserved time, but because it was in-family and his daughter needed him, he was given probation. The little one has put the pieces together and thinks her dad is at fault. She also knows that he drinks too much. It's a real problem here, isn't it?"

Francis had already noticed that when Jesus asked a question, it wasn't really a question but an affirmation of what he had just said. "Yes, it is," he said.

"Anyway, she's very angry with him because of what he did. He's in unit sixty-two."

He knew Mr. Darby who always gave him a tip at Christmas. He seemed nice enough, but he was always a bit tipsy. Sometimes he'd be waiting for his mail. Francis didn't like it when he'd be there by the mailbox in the hallway because he talked so much, especially after his wife died. It was obvious that he was mostly all alone with no one to listen to him. The man could talk your ear off about anything. Francis remembered once trying to get away from him after he had put the mail in the slots. He handed him his mail. Richard seemed to like that he was paying attention to him and giving him a sort of special status among the others by personally giving him his letters. He asked Francis how the weather was. He should have run from the lobby. He told him it was nice out, just right, a good breeze blowing. He must have told the mailman a hundred little stories about the weather. He was about a half-hour late finishing up that day.

"Jesus, you said that you offered a gift to him. Would you mind telling me about the gift?"

"Richard doesn't believe in anything. Ever since he was kid, he hasn't believed in anything. He's got reasons, all right. I guess we all do. His reasons are pretty powerful.

"If I were to ask you what person or persons in your life do you think you could count on to love you, what would you say?"

"I'd say my mother and father."

"I think you're right. Each person has some instinctive idea that their parents should protect them in the world. It's just the right thing. Richard got very mixed up about lots of things when his parents not only did not love him, but tortured him in some very sadistic ways. They did this to him when he was very young, a child.

"They sometimes would get drunk and hang him out by his feet from the fifth-floor apartment where they lived. The mother would take him by one foot and the father by the other and just hang the little guy out with his head down. He'd scream with fear, almost out of his mind. Then, when it got really bad, so that he was almost fainting, one of them would let go of the one foot, leaving him dangling by the other. They'd laugh and carry on before bringing him back into the room. Then they'd reprimand him because he was so angry with them. Often, they'd then slap him into resignation. 'Disrespectful child,' they'd say."

"I didn't know," Francis said.

"Well, of course you didn't, Francis. Not even his daughter, Erin, knows. He's very ashamed. I love him, especially love him because of what has happened. I'd like him to know that the stuff with his parents, the accident, his daughter's anger ... can melt away if he would only believe in his own goodness. I want him to have faith.

"He might be constitutionally incapable of loving himself. It's a hard sell with people who have been abused. It really gets into their cells that they're bad people and deserve what has happened to them.

"I've been trying to get him to know this, but he just doesn't believe it. What he does makes things worse with Erin. He's just not there for her. It's not that he's a bad father. He loves her but doesn't interact with her. He doesn't say goodbye when she leaves for school and doesn't say hi when she comes home. Even when he tries to do something with her, it's always about him. He'll ask her if she wants to go to the movies, then pick the one he wants to see. He's just not present. The alcohol makes it worse. I know that it diminishes how he thinks about himself. When he drives his car, he thinks he's invisible, so he has to be extra careful at traffic lights and stop signs.

"Here's where you come in. I'll be talking with him in the letters you'll deliver. There's more to it, but so much for now."

He seemed preoccupied, as if he had something else to do. Then he said, "Francis, I know it can be a bit heavy being with me, so I want to tell you ahead of time how I leave so I don't scare you. I just disappear. Poof!"

And he just disappeared. The clock in the kitchen read 8:35.

8

He was surprised when Ellen called with an unusual request. Seemed that Thomas had developed an interest in hockey. She said he had begun to watch the Rangers' games on TV and had asked her to buy him an interactive video game put out with the blessings of the National Hockey League. He loved to play against his brother Kyle, who, she said, was no match. He even asked his mom to get him roller skates, a hockey stick, and a roll of black sticky tape that he could use as a puck to shoot against the brick wall around the corner. He was starting to spend Saturday mornings at a quiet side block one stop away on the elevated trains (the El), where there was a teenage street hockey league. He idolized the players and often referred to one of the goalies called "Scotty" by the other boys.

He'd come home, she said, and tell her that Scotty did this and Scotty did that, kick saves and beauties, like he was one of the professional superstar goalies. She was concerned about the hero worship, that it would get in the way of Thomas's self-esteem, that he ought to be spending his time studying instead of playing video hockey games.

"I want you to take him to a game," she said. It was not so much a request as it was a directive. She's gotten like that once the divorce proceedings started, as if Francis was to blame.

She felt some kind of moral superiority that began to play itself out in how she spoke to him. The tone of her requests shifted toward being mandates.

"What game?" he asked.

"A hockey game," she answered with a sigh. He could see her rolling her eyes.

"What hockey game?" he asked as innocently as possible with a dash of bewilderment.

"The Rangers' game," she answered irritably. Now she would be rubbing her neck and rolling her entire head. He knew he could ratchet up this kind of verbal ping-pong they played.

What he was feeling was a put-down. It'd be better if she asked him instead of telling him. If he said that to her, though, she'd respond with one or another complaint. That he never did anything with the kids, that if she left it up to him the boys would never get to a game. On and on. It wasn't worth it, so when she got like this, he backed off.

"Okay," he said, "but how do you get tickets?"

She was ready for the back and forth games he played. "The poor, innocent one," she called it, a way of getting out of doing some of the work in the marriage. He'd say he didn't know how to do this or that, then she'd do it. Easy.

"I've already got three tickets for next week at the Garden. I want you to bring Kyle too. If you don't, he'll feel left out."

"I suppose," was all he said.

"Next Thursday," she said. "Be here at 5 p.m., and don't be late. The game starts at 7:30, and that will give you plenty of time."

The first few months after the divorce were terrible for Francis. Every time Ellen and he would talk, she'd pull out stuff about what a deficient person he was. He didn't know why divorced women did this, but a couple of guys he know went through the same thing. After a while, he began to feel lousy about himself. The only defense was to talk to her only when necessary.

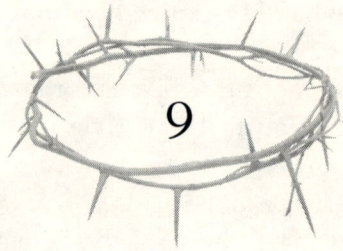

9

Jesus was a really good communicator. He sent Francis a letter every time he wanted to see him, probably because he didn't want to scare him by showing up unannounced. He received this letter from him a few days before he was to see Thomas and Kyle.

Dear Francis,

I was going to meet with you this coming Thursday evening. But Ellen wants you to take the boys to a hockey game that night. So, let's meet tomorrow night instead. It's very important that we talk before you go to the hockey game because something you think is bad might happen at the game, something that is related to why I have been talking with you. Same time.

Love,
Jesus

The weird thing about this letter was that Francis got it the day before Ellen and he talked about the game on the phone. This time, he waited in his apartment and left the blue chair for Jesus, just in case he was a creature of habit.

"I'm not a creature of habit, Francis. Nor am I a creature. A creature is someone created by my Father. I am not exactly created, even though it appears that I am. I am God. I always existed in the mind of my Father. From all eternity, from always. It is a concept hard for humans to understand. I mean that I have not been created but have always been in my Father's mind.

"You also, Francis, have been always in my Father's mind. As is every person who has ever lived on this planet. It is a far more powerful reality to be in the beloved's mind than is understood. Most of you seem to want evidence that you can hold in your hand. A body of evidence, so to speak."

It sounded like Jesus was making a joke. Even though Francis found what he said funny, he didn't know if he should laugh. It wasn't like he was a stranger giving a lecture with a joke or two thrown in. He was God, sitting in his apartment, in his chair, talking to him. It was personal. To laugh would be a sort of intimacy, perhaps unwanted.

It was obvious that Francis was nervous to see him. Things were starting to rev up about why he was there, and he didn't know where it was going. He figured a little small talk might be relaxing.

"I made spaghetti for us, if that's okay with you. I

know you like Chinese, but I didn't know if two times in a row would be good. I figured I'd mix it up a bit."

"Spaghetti will be very good. But let's talk first. You know that I am here to ask you to help with something special to me and to my Father." He nodded. What he said next startled him.

"I met last night with the Heavenly Council about your readiness for this undertaking. They thought unanimously that you are not ready. Arland Williams was especially vocal. He is committed in his belief that until a person is ready to do something courageous, we cannot expect him to do it. He told the group about a powerful urge that had been growing in him for years to do something good and helpful to those around him. And he accepted that if he ever did do anything generous for anyone that the ripples of his influence would be small and tidy. Of course, what he did, giving up his life for others in the plane crash, was big time."

Jesus seemed to be thinking again—olive skin wrinkled above his brows, lips pursed pensively. No matter what or how many times he explained to Francis that he was here in a powerful human way, he always found it kind of amusing, maybe puzzling, that he appeared to think before he spoke.

"I am not yet going to tell you everything about why I am here. For now, it is enough for you to know that the people to whom I am asking you to deliver letters will be involved with you." Then he added, "In the extreme.

"So you are not simply the man who delivers letters.

You are involved in the content of the letters. I suggest that you get to know these people as best you can."

Francis wanted to say *Holy mackerel,* but of course, he did not. Instead, he said, "You told me on your last visit that I would be delivering letters to several people. Yet, you have only told me about two of them.

He asked Jesus if he would like to tell him over the spaghetti he had made the night before. "It's second-day spaghetti, the best kind. I'll heat it in the microwave and put a little butter on the sauce, if you'd like." He liked the idea, and Francis got right with it.

He spoke as they ate. "Bill Waxman is 88 years old, unit 43, a gentle man. Hard to believe when you know that he's killed forty men. Japanese. Ironically, he thinks a lot about death now. When he was twenty-five on Iwo Jima, he hardly gave it a thought. He convinced himself that he was immune. Even when he saw his buddies get blown apart.

"I'll tell you a story about him. He went to a high school in Connecticut. Bethel High School. It was a small bedroom town. Still is, for the most part. His best friend got engaged in senior year to a very sweet young lady, a really good girl.

"When it was time to go to war, Bill and his buddy Ned signed up together to join the U.S. Marines. Bill always said that Ned was the best man he ever knew. He even told people that on several occasions when he shook his hand a jolt of electricity ran right through his arm. It was my Father's love for Ned.

"They were assigned to the same unit. They fought in the same battles: Saipan, Tinian, Iwo, although they rarely saw each other. Bill was in communications, a runner who was out front all over the islands, rolling and stringing telephone wire right up to the Japanese caves. He was a sitting duck. Never got hit, though. A nick here and there, Purple Heart stuff, but nothing big.

"Ned was a medic, a truly fine and heroic one. He considered every Marine on Iwo, where he was killed, to be his buddy. Whenever he heard a yell for help, nothing could stop him. To this day, Bill thinks about the irony of being right next to him when he was killed in a fierce firefight near the end of the battle. Bullets were zipping past their heads, pinging on rocks and pieces of equipment. Bill tried to convince Ned to stay behind a cluster of boulders when a string of voices, first here, then there, left, right, screamed 'Medic, Medic.'

"'Just wait a few minutes 'til things die down,' Bill pleaded with him. Of course, Ned wouldn't wait. A sniper's bullet went right through his open mouth. Bill thinks he was about to tell the wounded that he was on his way."

Francis didn't know why Jesus was telling him all this. But, then, he knew it had something to do with him, yet he couldn't figure out what.

"Bill killed lots of Japanese soldiers on Iwo Jima. But he thought of it as mercy killings, just going about from cave to cave finishing off the men who tried to commit suicide by blowing themselves up with hand grenades.

"He was like almost every other young soldier. He

was just doing his duty for his country. But Ned's death was the start of erosion in whatever faith Bill might have had in anything. Eventually, he stopped going to church and became very cynical about authority. While all this was festering, he started to read about the war he had fought in. He started to think that Ned and the rest of them were fodder, just fodder. Especially when research material began to come out that it might be a myth that twenty thousand aviators were saved by landing on Iwo in the months prior to the end of the war, and that many of the planes were not necessarily in dire trouble, that the island was a convenience, but not a necessity.

"Bill has allowed this thinking to become like rust on his soul. He's been drying up for about fifty years now. Believes in nothing anymore, except maybe his great-granddaughter, little Megan, who lives nearby. She's about eleven. He visits her as often as he can because he knows that he sees in her, and only in her, the possibility that life once was for him.

"Megan is special," Jesus continued. "We knew this when she was born. But she has really built on the gifts she inherited. And she often says *yes* to the gifts my Father offers to her. It is such a difficult place for youngsters living now in this country, on this planet. So many temptations.

"Bill is a good man, and Megan is a gift to him. She gives him hope that life is worthwhile. We think it is sad and good what is happening to him. Obviously sad when someone loses his bearings, but good when he realizes that killing each other is not the most effective way to handle these matters. You have been killing for thousands of years without letup. The problem with Bill's realization is that he doesn't think he has any way to convince others of it."

All of this about Bill Waxman was good to know, yet Francis couldn't see how it fit in with him or what problem there might be at the hockey game Thursday night.

"Jesus, you said in your note that something bad might happen at the hockey game I'm taking the boys to. I'm interested in hearing about Mr. Waxman's problems, but I don't see how getting to know him has any bearing on my life. Frankly, for the moment I am not as interested in him as in what might happen at the game. If it's not too much to ask, would you kindly explain?"

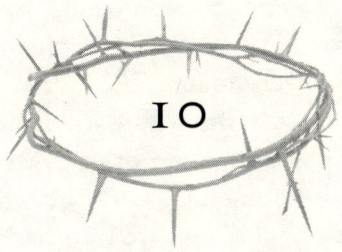

10

"I told you before that the Heavenly Council doesn't think you are ready yet to hear what I would like to tell you. I know that, but I have seen your potential to be ready. So, for the moment, let's just begin." He looked at the mailman in a way that no one had ever before. The look was not strange, nor weird. Not spooky, nor frightening. It was penetrating. Like he was looking into his soul and could see the absolute truth of it. The look took away all the subterfuges, the deceit, and the lies he sometimes told himself without even knowing it. He could see who he was.

"Francis, do you love Thomas and Kyle?"

"I love them very much," he answered without hesitation.

"No," he said, "let me say it again. I didn't ask you 'how much do you love them?' I asked you, 'Do you love them?'"

"Well, of course I love them. They are my boys."

"Good. That's good," Jesus said. "Now, let's move this ahead. How much do you love them?"

"I love them very much," he said.

He could hardly hear him when he said, again, "Good, that's good." After a brief pause, which Jesus spent staring into Francis's eyes, he again spoke. "I suppose you know that you are transparent to me?"

"I don't know what that means."

"It means I can see everything that's in your soul, in your heart. It means I can see every reservation you might have in answering my questions, even though you might speak in a way that says otherwise."

"Yes, I believe it's like that."

"So don't knee-jerk answer to me based on what you think I expect or what your upbringing tells you to say."

He didn't know why he was so comfortable with Jesus. He felt like he really knew him, as they say, all his life. You'd think he might not know what to do or say right now. What he knew was to do nothing, to say nothing.

Jesus's voice was somber. "Francis." Again, he seemed like he was thinking of what to say next. Instead, he said to him, "Francis, why are you laughing?"

"Oh, Jesus, I didn't mean to laugh. What I mean is I'm not laughing at you. I just think it's funny what came into my mind."

"And what was it that came into your mind?"

Now he was really confused. "Didn't you tell me

that I am transparent to you? If it's that way, why do you ask?"

Jesus seemed to sigh, and immediately Francis thought that he had over-stepped his bounds.

"Can't you see that I'm trying hard to be human here? Don't you know by now that if I wanted to act like God that we wouldn't even be talking. I could be pulling the strings—yes, pulling the strings, I said. I'm even trying to talk like you. 'Pulling the strings.' I'm not saying 'exercising my omnipotence' or 'recanting my commitment to free will.' I'm saying 'pulling the strings.'"

He seemed sad at what had just happened. Francis wanted to console him. But he was Jesus, still dressed in that long, flowing, and somewhat grungy robe, yet he did feel something special for him. And he liked him.

"Look, Francis," he said, "I'm going to tell you something. When my Father asked me to come down here to be a human being, he really wanted to shake up the world. He wanted to let people know how much they meant to him, that he wasn't some kind of thunderclap they should worship, or make sacrifices to, like he was some kind of god. He's God. They got it all wrong. The Father does not need sacrifices to him, or worship. He's not needy that way.

"I know it might sound corny to you, but I'm going to say it in the way that I think you will understand. My Father is all about love. And because of the way he and I decided I'd be here on earth, I too am all about love, in ways that I hope you can understand. It is rare that a human is capable to know the fullness of what it means to love the way he loves. Maybe Arland comes the closest.

"If you took the most self-centered man in the world and put all that energy into loving—not himself but another... No, better, if you took the man who loves his beloved more than life itself, and I'm happy to tell you there are such men, and you knew what he knew about his love for her, then multiply that love by the biggest number a computer can generate, you would still fall short of knowing how the Father loves. You would never grasp the biggest number."

He didn't know what to say to that. He tried. "Jesus, I do love my children."

"I know you do. That's why you're not going to like what I have to say."

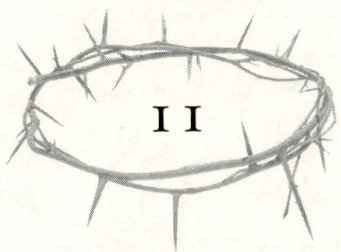

I I

It took Jesus a while before he thought Francis was ready to hear what he wanted to tell him. He explained that we use the word *sometimes* to mean every now and then. It was really a way, perhaps unknown to us, that we ran in and out of regular time, in a goofy sort of way. That time, as we think we know it, is not real, just a way for us to keep the drumbeat regular, even when it's not regular, as in sometimes. He said we don't have much of a capacity to do it any other way. He wanted Francis to know that he would mostly keep to the clock, but every now and then he would not. That this was the best way for him to do the mission with him.

Now, you've got to understand how hard this was for Francis to comprehend since he really didn't know yet what the mission was. But, he was comfortable enough.

"I am God, but I am also a human being. I have

the capacity to be fully and totally a human being without the God in me taking over. The God in me does not enhance my ability as a person to love others. I've got to work at it just like you do."

"I know what you mean. I love my children, but their mother … you'll never know how hard that is for me. She has a way that makes me feel inferior. It's like something is missing in her that she finds only when she is putting me down."

"I do know how hard that is. It is the very thing I am talking about. Do you think that every time my wonderful father on earth, Joseph, asked me to help him with chores when I wanted to play with the other boys that I wasn't sore-pressed to stay back?

"Francis, please sit down. I should have told you this before. I know that the letters and my coming here is a very hard thing for you to understand. But, I know that you have the capacity. I know, too, in my humanity that it is sometimes difficult to speak about things that make us uneasy.

"I didn't want to let on to my mother about things to come. Every now and then, I'd mention the future, but not often. I knew she knew. It was just an understanding out of my love for her that I did not talk about it. You know how hard that would be on a mother, knowing that she was raising her son to be crucified. I mean, we had to live a regular life until it was ready for me to do what my Father asked."

God, how he loved Jesus right then.

"I know you do," he said.

"Francis, how about going on a walk? I know that

Queens isn't Nazareth, but it would do me good to stroll again."

"Let's walk up Grand Avenue to Steinway Street," Francis said, "the place where I deliver most of my mail. I think, though, we might have a problem. I don't want to hurt your feelings, if I could do that, but you're not exactly dressed for anonymity. I mean, you won't sink into the crowd."

"I see your point," Jesus said. "Lend me some clothes."

Then, as an afterthought, he looked Francis in the eye and said, "Please," before he asked him about the long beard. "It stays," he said without hesitation.

So there he was. Jesus in a pair of jeans, sneakers, plaid shirt, and New York Yankees windbreaker, walking the avenue with Francis. "How does it compare to Nazareth?" Francis asked, just as he was bumped by a young man trying to catch a bus. "Busy, noisy, but I like it. I like how the shops are small, how individuals make their living in the little shops. It's an honest way to be."

They walked to the main intersection, where at night from left to right and on both sides of the street, the string of small stores appeared to be bracelets of tiny lights made brighter by the overhanging street lights. Fruits, suits, dresses, ice cream cones, deli stuff, coffee, bagels, movie theaters. Anything you'd ever need.

"How about a real New York hotdog?"

"Don't mind if I do," Jesus said. He hadn't eaten much earlier but had apparently relocated his appetite. Two dogs with sauerkraut and mustard, and they were on their way.

They passed one of the large apartment buildings. "This is where I spend lots of my time delivering the mail," Francis explained to him. "In fact, the woman coming our way is one of my customers."

"Yes, I know."

Cora Aldrich was about forty. Francis thought she was naturally attractive, and it made him angry that she covered herself with so much makeup that her face had the look of a painted mannequin. "Hi, boys," she said. "How is my favorite mailman today?"

He wasn't sure if he should introduce her to Jesus. He knew certain things about her. "Hello," Jesus said, leaving him with no recourse.

"Mrs. Aldrich, this is my friend Jesus," he said before he realized that he should have first asked Jesus if he wanted him to use a different name. Too late. What he was afraid of was about to happen.

"Well, you don't look like Jesus," she said, a twinkle in her eye, like she had just made a joke worthy of notice.

Francis tried to cover up. "He's really *Hey-soos,* the Spanish, you know."

"Well, he doesn't look Spanish."

Jesus saved the day, saying "I'm pleased to meet you."

"Well, I'm very pleased to meet you," she said. "Maybe sometime we could get together. And you, big lug of mailman, next time I ask you to take a break and drop in for a little conversation, please do," she uttered in a way that was entirely too coy.

"How's the little girl, Mrs. Aldrich?" Francis

asked, trying to steer the conversation in a different direction.

"You know, Frank, I'd rather be called Cora." She took a breathing break, then said, "Call me Cora."

He was about to salute her to mock her directive, but said, "Yes, and how is Angelina?"

"She's fine. In fact, I'm taking her to the Garden this week. Hockey game."

He didn't dare tell her of his plans with the kids. If he did, she'd probably want to meet him there or something. "I didn't know you were a hockey fan," he said, even though he didn't care. Mrs. Aldrich was not his type.

"Ever since I was a kid," she answered. "Long-time big fan."

He didn't know about Jesus, but he had to get out of there. "Well, we've got to do a few things. See you on the road."

"It's my pleasure to meet you, Cora Aldrich," Jesus said in his most charming manner.

"And I you, Hey-soos," she giggled. "See you in church." Then, as if they didn't get the joke, she added in a slow drawl, "Jee-suss."

Maybe it was a need to impress Jesus, but Francis said to him as they continued to walk, "I'm sorry I screwed up there. We should have crossed the street and you wouldn't have had to meet her."

"I'm glad we met. She is one of the people you'll be delivering my letters to."

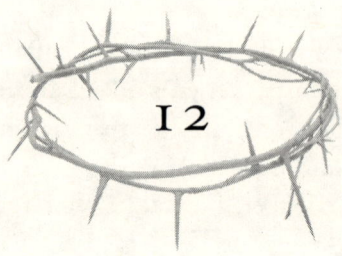

12

He was certain there is beauty in the world, though about goodness and truth he was not sure. He did see these things in Ellen when they were falling for each other. He knew, too, there was love; that is, until he took over and tried to run the whole show and ruined it all, the beauty, the truth, the goodness, the love. But on that night, walking down Steinway Street, his ability to love was more powerful than he had ever experienced it. He was being touched by Jesus. It was like a feeling of complete stillness and pure contentedness had taken him over.

"Jesus, I want you to know that Mrs. Aldrich is just a lady I deliver the mail to. She means nothing to me."

"But she ought to," he answered.

"I guess, but she's got a kind of reputation."

"Like a slut?"

"People talk about her always trying to pick up men, even though she's married. She always asks me to come into her apartment for a little tea or something." He paused so he'd get the implication.

"Francis, a minute ago you were experiencing a touch of what heaven is about. Just a tad. You are such a good man, yet you take on the attitudes of others so easily. Do you really know that Mrs. Aldrich is a slut? And if she is, what then?" He switched gears to focus now on Francis, who was growing uncomfortable quickly.

"But why is it no less important for you to be present to Cora Aldrich?"

When he stared off into another dimension, Francis couldn't help but wonder if he was back in heaven, just for a little while, perhaps to be re-energized with the spirit of his Father.

"Why does it seem like you're thinking about the past or the future when all time is now for you," he asked, interrupting Jesus's otherworldly state. "I mean, you could just have all of your experiences be now."

"It is a beautiful way that I can know my humanity, that I can tell what it is like to be a person. You don't seem to get that."

"I'm sorry. I'm just a little overwhelmed."

"Francis, there is such a goodness in you. How loving your heart can be. And your compassion."

All Francis could think of when he said these words was how his capacity to love had dwindled over the years, how his heart had grown cold. *I have failed him, and myself.*

"You have not failed me, Francis. But you could have pleased me more. You have grown listless and indifferent, especially toward your family, the greatest gift you have been offered. You once said *yes* to the offer, yet you did not take responsibility to water the garden.

"Please try very hard to hear me when I tell you that I am Jesus, a man. Maybe it is easier for me to be a good man. What I know is that my parents were holy and extraordinary. Certainly my father Joseph, unlike you, worked at being a father. It is said of him that he was a just man. Do you know what that means? It means that he gave to each person whatever was due to him. He gave fair wages to his carpenters, love and loyalty to my mother. And to me, well, he showed me the way to get prepared for what I had agreed to do.

"He gave, I took. When it was my turn, I gave, you and others took. I do not mind that. I welcome that."

As quickly as the conversation was getting heavy, it got light. "Let's cross over. I want to see that leather shop over there," he said, pointing to a small shop that featured sheepskin coats. He seemed excited. "I used to wear one of these in Capernaum where I lived with Peter's family, after I left Nazareth to begin preaching." He was holding a coat against his body, up against his torso as if imagining it on. After a few seconds, he replaced the garment and began strolling again. The excitement left his eyes, but a small smile still played on his lips.

They sat on a small bench near the far end of Steinway, near one of the movie theaters. "Would you like to go see a movie?" Francis asked, attempting something familiar.

"No," he answered. "I tried once, but didn't like it so much. Sorry to say, it seemed so unreal to me. Entertaining, but unreal.

"But this is good here, being together and watching the people go by. There's a nice feel here, a very nice feel. It's one of the reasons we chose Astoria. A good mix of hard-working people who try their best to be good people.

"Let me tell you about another person you will be delivering mail to. The last one. I know I have told you a lot tonight, but it is important for you to know these things before the hockey game Thursday. I hope I have not overburdened you.

"The man's name is Nicholas Street, unit ninety-three."

Francis's eyes widened and his words tripped over Jesus's in his excitement. "I know him. He's a nice guy. Great wife named Beverley. And a terrific kid named Aaron. He's about the same age as my Thomas."

"He's the one. What you don't know, and you are not to say anything about it unless he tells you, is that he has a brain tumor, and the doctors have given him nine months to a year."

"I'm sorry."

"I'm sorry, too," he said.

"I want to tell you about my Father and me. I must tell you now so you will be ready for what will happen at the hockey game. Ordinarily, it would take you years of experience to understand what I am going to say to you about the spirit. Saying *yes* to the gifts offered by my Father. Accepting the things you cannot change. Having the courage to change the things you can. That kind of stuff."

By this time, Francis was gulping hard, like he wished that Jesus never knew him. He was beginning to know when Jesus was warming up to something really big about life. It was like he had a personality, a way of looking at you and talking, a certain style that could be called a signature. He knew when Jesus was about to let him in on a secret or two. But, he wasn't always sure if he wanted to know. Here he was, trying to survive a divorce and make it on his own. These things were hard enough without Jesus coming into his life to tell him things he really didn't want to hear.

"Francis," he said ponderously, "do you know that you and I create the world together?"

Too much, Francis thought, *take me now.*

"No, I didn't," he wheezed.

"What I mean is that my Father created this world, among several other worlds. He wanted to trust humans to run it in a way that was good for each person and to keep passing it on. The goodness, I mean. In a very personal way—a very personal way," he repeated, "my Father creates every person special and different and places them in time at exactly the right moment he intends for them.

"I am also created by our Father to be unique, just like you. You've got to remember, though, that he created me also as a person. Be certain that he first asked me. He said it was a gift, a special gift that he was offering to me. I said, 'Yes, my Father, may thy will be done on earth as it is in heaven.'"

"But, how could it be a gift when you knew that you were going to be crucified? If I knew that was coming, I wouldn't think of it as a gift."

"I am of the Father. He is of me. I love the way my Father loves, you might say in the same way. It is a gift he offered me because if I said yes, I would also be human, something he does not have. You might think that he does not want to be human, though that is not the case. Let me say for now that, simply, he does not want. He simply is.

"In the way he has created me, I have created you, though, of course, you are not God. You are in the image of God. How extraordinary that you and I and my Father, as well as every person who has ever existed, co-create this world."

For just an instant, Francis understood what he was telling him. That he, and Ellen, Thomas, and Kyle, his fellow postal workers, were creators of the world as it is. *If that is so,* he thought, *then maybe we are not doing a very good job.*

"You know the world is a mess in lots of ways. Why don't you just take it over and have it your way?"

"It's not the way my Father wants it. If it was, then this world would be heaven. Like the days when all is well, when you're in touch with others, when you know in the deep places of your heart and mind that the world is okay. Dogs, cats, birds, deer, whales, elephants, butterflies, and on and on, and know that this place is good."

Of course, he knew what Francis was thinking right then.

"For now, I must only tell you that even babies, born with defects, are also perfect. A touch of heaven is when you realize the perfection and accept that it is a sign of what can be. It is when you accept yourself with all your faults and just know that it's part of the way it is since the garden of Eden.

"Whenever you know these things and you still carry on toward your goodness, then you and I and my Father co-create the world, along with everyone else in it. It is as if we are a liquid co-creativity. We water each other, my Father and I, you and I, my Father and you, you and everyone else. Do you know that each time you say yes to this process that we all move away from sin and toward what was intended? Others have done it, you know."

"Who has done it?" he wanted to know.

"There are other worlds, Francis. I know that might come as a surprise to you. A few of these worlds have evolved, you might say, as in the vision of my Father. A few have not. Others are on their way toward becoming. So, of course, you want to know about these worlds," he said. Just then, a homeless man came toward them, pushing a cart of his scant belongings. He looked at them and locked on the face of Jesus.

"Would you have anything to help out an old man?"

"Francis," Jesus asked, "do you have any money to give to this man?"

He gave him a dollar. The man seemed grateful. Before leaving, he and Jesus lightly smacked palms.

"So you want to know about other worlds? I will tell you."

Francis pinched himself.

"There are five other worlds ... to be exact. Four of them you might understand, because in many ways they are like the Earth. The other one you will not."

He wanted to hear about the one he wouldn't understand. He was about to ask Jesus when he said, "Let me tell you first about the place that is different. It is not a planet, not a planet like you know planets. It is beyond planets.

"Perhaps you know," he continued, "how scientists and philosophers love to guess about the boundaries of the universe, where space ends. I know that it is almost hypnotic to look into the night sky, especially on a clear night, and wonder about where it ends, and what is behind where it ends. When I was a young man traveling through the Judean desert, I would look into the night sky and sometimes beg my Father to tell me where it ends. He would not.

"In your world, in your way of thinking, there is always something behind where anything ends. At least you like to think so. The game ends, but there is always another game. Season over, but wait 'til next year. Marriage gone, but there will be another soul mate. Last dollar in the wallet, but hang on, the check will come. The last stop on the train is really not the end. War destroys, and you rebuild.

"You are right in many things, some of you wise in

many ways. The place I refer to is beyond the universe, though it is not heaven. It is more advanced than you know, but not yet heaven."

"Is it a place where only special people go because they have followed your word on Earth? Is it a reward? Is it Abraham's bosom?"

"No," he answered. "This place, which its inhabitants call Incarnata, is where everyone loves each other beyond what people here can imagine. Let us acknowledge that there are humans who love greatly and powerfully. It is as if they have tapped into the being of my Father. The ones who live on Incarnata would never even imagine doing things that are done on Earth.

"Yet, they do have a problem. I think it is a nice problem. They must learn to accept their loving nature without it killing their spirit."

"I'm sorry," Francis said in frustration, "but I just don't understand what you are telling me. How can someone love so much that they can... well, that it can kill their spirit? How can that be?"

"Their problem, if you want to call it that, is basic. If their spirit is deadened because they cannot accept their ability to love, they will be exiled. No, that word will give you the wrong idea. Not cast out or put in prison. The best way I can tell you is that they then become like you, in another place where they must learn from scratch, as you say, to love. Then, it is not like here where you have the capacity to love at the outset and must work to keep it and increase it."

"I *still* cannot understand how loving much can cause destruction of the spirit," he said.

"I can tell that you are annoyed, Francis, annoyed that you cannot understand these things. Maybe this will help. All of reality is made up of opposites. There is no up without a down, no win without a loss, no act of generosity without indifference, no good without evil."

He started to explain how evil was the absence of good. It was getting too much for Francis. "Jesus, please, I beg you now … Jesus Christ! I am sorry, but I am just a regular man, not so smart, but not dumb. But always, always I cannot take too much at once. Would you kindly tell me about the other worlds?"

He wanted to go to sleep, back to the boring life he led. He didn't know why Jesus was telling him all of this, and he started to not want to know. It was becoming a burden to know so much, especially since he couldn't tell anyone without them thinking he was crazy.

"I know that in spite of yourself, you are insatiably curious. When you are able, we will return to this topic.

"The other four planets are now, finally, at peace. I don't mean with each other, as none of them, except one, has any awareness of the existence of the others. They do not war anymore. All weapons have been abolished, even guns that were once used to kill animals."

"What do they eat if not cows and sheep and … "

"They do not eat pigs and chickens, either." He

finished the thought. "These planets also live at peace with animals. There are enough fruits, vegetables, and greens to sustain life. When the inhabitants finally understood that it is a better way to not eat the animals, that they could live longer and without cancers of every sort this way, they began to believe in meat abstinence.

"I will admit that these planets have a head start. On the planets I speak of, there is one season, a perfect one. Growing food is not a problem. And it is equally distributed, with order. There is no need for oil any more, as they have perfected the science of physical displacement; what you call 'teleportation.' No cars, busses, trains, or planes. Generally, the rule is that you can be teleported if the distance is over one mile.

"They don't even abuse the forests. There is no need. As I have told you, the climate is perfect."

Wow! he thought. He also thought, *No fair.* Yet, he didn't say anything.

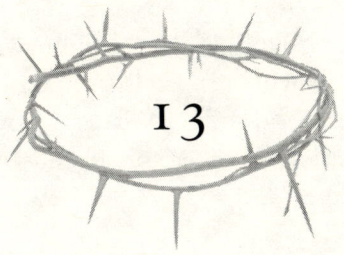

13

ELLEN

Growing up in Astoria, Queens, was so easy for Ellen that she never developed whatever a girl needs to combat boredom, though she was, in fact, boring. The quality seemed to be coded into her genes, which, in time, nurtured themselves into lions guarding the gates that led to self-awareness.

Ironically, there wasn't a lot to guard. She first realized that she was a cute blond in seventh grade when Vincent asked her to be "his girl." What she didn't know was that there were millions of cute blonds in the world, and probably hundreds, maybe thousands, within a city mile of the apartment where she lived with her parents. But it was a big deal to be asked, especially as the request itself was a sort of naughty stepping out. At Our Lady of Mt. Carmel elementary school, any gesture that might infer a dis- tinction between genders was looked upon as suggestive, depending on the degree of suspicion that lurked in each nun who might govern a school grade.

Being seen together as a couple was about the same as being celebrities, each time an event to anyone who was blessed to be a witness. Long before the arrival of paparazzi, family and friends were eager to take their picture and to revel in how precious were the images.

That it was Vincent who asked her was also a sign to her circle of how special she was. Vincent's father was a doctor, some kind of baby doctor, it was thought, though his practice was not in Astoria. It might as well have been in Hong Kong.

In a world of shabby shirts, Vincent came to school each day wearing a white shirt and tie, creased pants, and polished shoes. His intelligence, calculated and predictable, matched his wardrobe. He received high marks, always, except on an occasional essay question in history which might press itself against his imagination. Rarely did this place him at a disadvantage, as these types of questions were only occasionally asked as a relief from the rote, which was his specialty. Mostly, though, it was the impression left by his father's status that gave prestige to Vincent, and then, of course, to Ellen.

By the end of high school, during which time Vincent held tight to her and on one occasion in her, the cocoon unraveled. He was off to pre-med in Syracuse, where the temperatures would occasionally match his personality, and she to a clerk's position at the local Woolworth's, which was where she met

Francis. Although their courtship was not much different in most ways from others, there was a certain uniqueness about it.

"Ellen, we've been going out with each other for six months now, and all we have ever done is kiss on the cheek." He waited a moment for the implications of what he had just said to sink in. "Well," he said, "I don't know how to tell you this, but I need more." As they were lying under a tree at Astoria Park, and under the umbrella of a night sky, he seized the moment by grabbing her butt and pulling her toward himself. At the same time, overcome by his constant preoccupation with what such a moment might be like, he seized her hair in his balled-up fist and thrust his tongue into her mouth, to no avail.

He was usually such an unresponsive young man that it didn't take her long to disembowel what little actionable passion he had. The incident served as a reminder to her of how she had once allowed young Vincent to penetrate her, with all the subsequent anxieties about getting pregnant and losing status with family, friends, and neighborhood gossips, who would forever frame her reputation as one of the sluts who lived on the block.

Over time, Ellen realized that Francis was all she had between the appealing image she had of herself and the reality that each young man she dated between breakups with him wanted nothing less than quick sex. It was clear what they were after, and since she really was not a dumb blond, they were not going to get it. In fact, she was not very interested in that part of life.

Francis's continued interest in his fantasy of her undressed and ready was a sort of rubbery glue that kept bouncing them back to each other and holding them together for short periods of time. The reactivations of their relationship built up a sort of critical mass that would eventually explode into her agreeing to marry him, if he asked. By the time he was finally courageous enough to ask and to accept her expected rejection of a proposal, she settled and did say, "Yes."

From the day of the marriage, really the night of it, things began to go wrong. It was to be expected. Although he was a good man in the general sense of not being a hurtful man, Francis did not know much about himself. His parents had trained him to mute whatever in his core might have an urge to be heard. This was accomplished by screams and shouts, and sometimes by long periods of withdrawals and silence. In Francis's case, the unpredictability of it all was enough to shut him down. It is what he brought into the marriage.

On the first of its many dreary days, he was as happy as he could remember. There she was, Ellen, golden girl all dressed in white, a ripe plum ready for Francis to eat. Yet, on that first night, he didn't get even as much as a small bite.

"Francis," she reprimanded him, "you seem more interested in the money we received today than you are in me." He was sitting on the bed that could have been the marital bed, hardly reading the good-will cards before piling up the cash in groupings of ones, fives, tens, twenties and even a few hundreds.

"I've got some loot here," he said to her. Maybe it was because he hadn't included her as one of the beneficiaries that she determined right then that he would have no part of her that night.

She stalled as much as she could before he would ask the inevitable question, "How about a little?" Her answer would set a tone for the marriage.

"A little what?" A question which, at least she thought, would make him fess up his dirty thoughts about her, not realizing that his thoughts weren't as much about her as they were about any woman who might give him access, something his shy reserve would never allow him to seek. Being married to Ellen was, in some ways, a sort of getting it where he could.

"You know," he stammered, no more steady in groping for the right word as he would have been touching her, had she allowed. There was no lead-up with Francis, though, no training, no way of being that was his that could have allowed him to be coy with her.

"If it's sex you're after, you won't get it with me, not tonight."

Normally, it would take something special for Francis to lose his cool. A hammer blow that missed the nail and found his finger. More than once he had been put on notice for overreacting to a postal client who yelled at him for being late with the mail when it was not his fault. Yet tonight he felt like he had a right to her, and that his rights were being violated.

"Come on, take off your clothes," he almost demanded. Then, he got stupid. "I want to go for a ride," he told her. She was a city girl and knew what that meant.

Then she got cruel and lied. "I've got my period."

Given his repressive upbringing, he reacted to this with the utmost respect. *Never mess with the rag,* he had been taught. *Never.* With the sound of air slowly leaving a leaky balloon, he quietly and simply uttered, "Oh." He brushed his teeth, took off his clothes except his undershirt and jockey shorts, then got under the covers in bed beside her. There she was, six inches from him, yet she might as well have been a thousand miles away. It was a moment, had he known what the future with Ellen might be like, that could have been a metaphor for their marriage.

Sleep usually came easy to Francis. But on that night it did not. Rejection was never an easy thing for him to bear. The idea of it as a possibility always lurked in the background of his relations with females. He loved them, and he feared them. And when he most yearned for them, he felt most afraid that he might be consumed by the flat nothingness of their rejection, a veto of his will to step out. At times like this, he felt like a man parched, whose only recourse to satisfy his thirst was to jump naked into a body of water filled with floating ice.

He would not stand for that on his wedding night. With his body still throbbing, he finally worked up his courage once more and asked if she was still awake. When she didn't answer, the throbbing moved to his brain. "Dammit, Ellen, tonight was supposed to be my night." And then, in a last sputtering before going to sleep, he said in a kind of melodramatic tone, "If not tonight, then tomorrow."

He rose with the sun, but could do no better than rub against her while spooning. She angrily told him later that day that she felt trapped by his arms wrapped around her, that she felt she could do nothing. And how would he like to wake up with a blob of goo all over his new nightclothes? *Assault* was the word she used. At first, she thought of calling it *rape*, but, in the name of their less-than-a-day-old marriage, she did not.

Needless to say, the rest of their honeymoon was spent over silent candlelight dinners, afternoons at the beach reading, and evenings playing checkers and watching TV. In a dim sort of way, they both recognized the fog that was to creep in as droplets over the years. They knew without knowing that they had very little to bring to the table. Vaguely, they knew that married partners spoke with each other and sometimes did things together that they might, at least in retrospect, talk about. That married couples were supposed to be more than casual friends.

Perhaps it was this small peek into what might be that moved them on the last night, before resuming their welcomed work routine, to conceive Thomas, the same boy that Jesus had his eye on as a catalyst to transform Francis into a man who could believe, a man who might leap beyond his intellect.

There would be drama for Francis in all of this,

and an even greater problem for Thomas. Jesus knew that Francis was capable of a great faith in the same way that the Father knew Abraham was capable of placing Isaac in his tender and loving care.

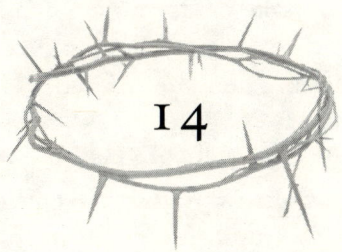

14

TINA AND JOE

Living in unit twenty-nine was fitting for Tina Remsen, a ten-year fixture at the Astoria General Library. A *magna cum laude* graduate of Queens College, she took the job right after getting her degree, though she was always clear to point out to friends that she was a librarian only in a generic and convenient sense, since her degree was in computer technology.

She liked living in the moderately small city apartment that also housed her husband, Joe, and their young son, Christopher. Its size accommodated her lifestyle. The kitchen was big enough to fit her cooking needs, which were small. She believed in the microwave. They had two bedrooms and once thought about getting a rabbit as a pet. She tried to make it sound like the rabbit could be a cat.

"You know, Joe, we could house-train him so he could have the freedom of the place." That seemed a little weird to Joe, who wanted to know where the *little thing* would take his training when he had to go.

"I thought we'd set up his poop box in the bathroom." Joe stared. Then she offered, "How about in the kitchen?"

If Tina had paid a little closer attention to Joe, she would have been aware that the bathroom was his reading room. You might even say, on some days, his library, if you measured the amount of time he spent there. As for the kitchen, "The kitchen is a place for food. Never mix our food with poo," he yelled at Tina with an extreme overstatement of the possibilities.

"Keep your voice down," is all she said, knowing for the umpteenth time that her wishes for a little diversion in the angles where the three of them bumped into each other was about to be aborted again.

Tina believed in the Bible and in the existence of heaven. Joe didn't believe in the Bible. He had read somewhere that the New Testament wasn't even "published," as he liked to think of its availability, until some four hundred years after the death of its protagonist, Jesus. *If the book is so true,* he asked himself, *why did it take so long for the truth to be revealed?* He was a skeptic.

She wasn't. In fact, she read the Bible every evening while Joe watched TV, warming it up, he thought. He liked to picture himself as a man who met his wife's needs, whatever those needs were. In practice, his best lights suggested to him that putting out the garbage and periodically going to the all-nighter to get a quart of milk for their morning coffee were major contributions to family togetherness.

Christopher copied his father's attitudinal stinginess and met his mother's demands to help out with one of many *non sequiturs*. His favorite was, "I didn't ask to be born." She once whispered to him, in a way that he interpreted as either sarcasm (often a port of call in her verbal knee-jerks to his response to life) or reality, that she also never asked to be born. Of course, he asked her what she meant by the remark.

"Probably the same as you mean," she answered. That really confused him.

Tina also believed in heaven. For a while, she even went to church on Sundays. In time, though, Joe's excuses for not going with her were too much to bear. Early NFL starting time, fatigue from his job as a stock supervisor at the A&P, up late with *Saturday Night Live*. Of course, Christopher figured out that whenever he wanted to do anything with his dad that his mom would latch onto his desires. Staying up late with dad was a sign that at least the father-son part of family togetherness was working.

In time, the church-going stopped altogether. Her loner personality had led to only acquaintances at service. The failure to find friends, the reluctance of "the boys" (as she liked to call her husband and son) to join her, and the shallow sermons that never reached her level of sophistication, one at a time, then altogether, became the nails that pegged her to the cross of her own alienation from the church.

In the early years, before Joe was a total jerk, when

she tried to explain to him about heaven, he wouldn't laugh at her, though she knew that was his reaction underneath to what he called her "childish notions built from sugary stories and movies." He just flat-out had no tolerance for her way of thinking, but with little skills to work with, he did not know how to tell her. He would "meet her needs" by listening for a few minutes before finding an excuse to stop, the same way he handled paperwork inventory on the job. He couldn't bear to think of heaven as a place where the weather was always good, where there were no bills, no worries. *Silly stuff,* he thought. Whenever Tina might ask him about his notions of heaven, he had more paperwork to do.

He began to think of his wife as being a silly girl. It was at this point that he turned into a total jerk. Once, she had the temerity to let him in on a very private thing, an insight, she called it, that God loved her as much as he loved anyone. She told Joe that she thought God might be a woman, knowing all the while that this confidence would bottle him up, perhaps for weeks.

"How could God love you as much as anyone else?" He was so infuriated with her arrogance that he got on one of his seizures, as Tina liked to call his non-stop lectures.

"You mean to tell me that he loves you as much as he loves the saints?" She wasn't sure what he meant as he then banged himself on the side of his head, muttering, "Jesus, Mary, and Joseph, this I can't believe."

If he meant to question that God loved her as

much as J, M, and J, she was ready to explain how that was so, that his love is indivisible, universal, and transcendent. She was that smart, and could talk that way, no matter the best thinking of theologians, mystics, or what have you.

Really, all she wanted to do was to share some of herself with him. He just sat in one of the kitchen chairs and stared into space, the space of what it might be like if he was married to a conventional woman who knew this from that, right from wrong, separated wisdom from her own silly thoughts. *God loves her as much as he loves anyone!*

As time went by and Tina realized that she and Joe were denizens of separate intellectual and emotional worlds, she tried extra hard to patch up their differences, usually by rendering service to him. "Would you like a cup of hot tea, Joe?" she asked in a soft and conciliatory tone one afternoon. He liked the tint of her voice at times like this because he thought it meant that he was the winner. He always thought he was the winner when she got like this. He always thought her attempts at harmony meant surrender. What he didn't know was that this minute on this day marked a new turn for a relationship gone stale.

"Do you know, Joe," she suddenly boomed like a thunderclap without warning, "that I don't give a crap if you want a cup of hot tea or not. If you do, get it yourself."

Joe was a bit taken back by the forcefulness of her remark, but not by much. "What do you mean by that?" he asked. Then, wanting to show how cool he was, he got up and went, tea kettle in hand, to the sink, where he turned on the coldwater tap and let it run for what seemed to be minutes.

"You're wasting water," she barked.

"We've gone over this about a million times," he answered back. "Cold water is more pure and makes a better cup. Now why don't you just leave me alone?"

"Sure, Joe," she said as he put on the burner. "Sure, Joe," she repeated, "I'll leave you alone." *Good*, he thought back.

"I'll leave you alone so you'll know what it's like for me to be alone," adding, "which I am, most of the time. I'll leave you alone so you'll know what the souls in hell feel when it's time. I'll leave you alone so you'll know what Christopher feels like to not have a dad." Just as she was about to reel off another *I'll leave you alone*, the kettle sang a hissy song. In the moment between when Joe poured the pure hot water onto a tea bag and pumped it up and down a few times like he was drilling for oil, Tina decided to let it all hang out.

"Where in God's name," she demanded, "do you get off telling me I can't have a rabbit? Who in hell do you think you are?" She shocked herself. It was the first time in their marriage that she had so mightily revealed her anger with him.

Joe was also shocked and a little apprehensive. He did not want to mess with a woman in anger, especially now. This was a different Tina. He thought it best to finish steeping the bag of tea, sugar the cup, and sit down. He knew that she had broken through his passivity, that she had touched the untouchable part of him, and he began to feel agitated.

A sort of black and white kind of guy, he read her question like an ultimatum: give in to her or get out, as in divorce. The idea had passed through his mind now and again, but like water through a sieve. Today, the idea became stuck in the gunk of their relationship. In that one loud and exact question, the years of disengagement from each other hit home.

As he sat down, he began to ask himself what life might be like without Tina and Christopher. At the same time, more like a tsunami of complete awareness than a stream of consciousness, Tina entertained, for the first time, what life would be like without Joe. *It would be good,* she thought. It would be hard, but she could probably get by. Her salary at the library was decent. And she probably could get a divorce judge to make Joe pay for Christopher's upkeep, at least for a while. Money wouldn't be a problem, she realized, until a deep blush of spiritual shame suddenly came over her for even thinking about these things.

The shame was to be expected, she realized, a price to pay for having always been sincere about the integrity of her marriage. One could not just break through a shell of conformity without at least blinking or rubbing one's eyes before looking at the new world. She had seen enough, though, for the first glimpse into her new world. But just as she was beginning to reproach herself for her thoughts, she knew that she had a right to a better life, a more compatible partner. There was a clarity in this that almost threw her against the fortress walls of her heritage and her parents, who proudly crowed to anyone who might listen that no one in their family, as far as they could tell, had ever been divorced.

This was much to bear, she realized. Not only would she have to tangle with the explosion of her personal ideals about family, but she would have to think about whether young Christopher could live on the other side of the happily-ever-after dream. Her parents, she knew, would not make it easier for them and might well infect her son with poisons about their daughter's disgrace.

The inner feeling of strength she got that day in the kitchen did not surprise her. She always knew that she was a strong woman, a reed standing tall, bending but never breaking.

"I didn't tell you not to get a rabbit. I merely pointed out that I didn't want it to crap in the bathroom or the kitchen," Joe murmured, just loud enough to be heard and to break her reverie.

"Oh," she uttered, happy at first that his response to her attack was muted. However, a tight boundary had been crossed, a wall torn down. As far as she was concerned, she had gone to the other side of some great and unspoken understanding between herself and Joe about the rules that he wrote to govern the family. "I don't give a crap about whatever it is that you say you said." The way of speaking was new to her and to Joe, although she knew that she had rehearsed the moment a hundred times in her head over the years.

"What I do give a crap about is that I'm tired of the lopsided ways we run this house. And I'm tired of the way you always make fun of me and my thoughts. Whenever they are different than yours, you make fun. But you're so dumb that you don't even know I just made a grammar mistake. You think you're so high and mighty about everything around here. Well, I'm about sick and tired of it."

He just sat there, sipping his tea. This was new territory for him, and he didn't know how to react. As that was so, he figured he'd stay cool and sip. After a few sips, he figured, Tina would go back to her old ways. He estimated that she would suffer great shame because of the level of her outburst, which would keep his sovereignty intact and unquestioned for about the next two years. That was her usual response whenever she got even a little outside herself.

He just kept sipping and sipping, waiting for her apology. Instead, Tina hunched low over him, looked him in the eye, and said, "Joe, I've got a notion to take this cup of hot tea right now and shove it down your throat."

If it wasn't comedic, it would be sad to watch him stand up, unclip the front of his suspenders, and take off his outer shirt before placing it neatly on the back of the chair. He re-clipped the suspenders before moving toward her as close as he could in order to stick his bare chest into her face. *This would show her who's boss,* he thought.

But he didn't realize that the equation had changed. Tina took both straps of his red suspenders in her hands as though she was transformed into a maniac bull drawn by the color and pulled them as far and fast as she could before letting go. The sound of the snap on Joe's chest was slightly lower than the howl from his mouth.

He lunged back in shock—more from the fact that Tina was capable of such an act than from the pain. All he could think to say was, "And you think that God loves you as much as anyone?"

"Yes, Joe, he does. And before today, I thought he loved you as much as he does me and Christopher. But now I'm not sure anymore."

He was deeply offended by the remark, realizing that to entertain her truth was to agree that God might love each one of us as much as the other. And for some mysterious and quirky way of the human heart, he tried now to win her over. He didn't know what he was trying to win her over to. After all, they didn't have an argument about any specific point— the rabbit or where it might defecate. It was more a heated discussion, he figured, about how things got done around here. That being the case, he began to plot how he could at least normalize things between them before he could once again win.

"That hurt," he said. "Seriously."

He would, though, realize before the tea was over that things in him had also changed. It was as if she had just nicked a festering wound, allowing the home- made poisons that had been building up in him over the years to be released. He tried to be nice, but he bore the cumulative effect of this disposition toward her as an indignity to his manhood. Something in him kept saying that this is not the way that things are to be done. He knew it would be better if he simply spoke the words and, in doing so, healed her soul from its insistent ways.

"How's it feel to get a little taste of your own medicine?" she asked. She wanted to get him something, anything, from the medicine cabinet to soothe the two puffy, reddish lines that immediately began to form on either side of his chest. She resisted, though it was almost a miracle that her maternal instincts, so finely inspired in her genes at the conception of her being, did not rush to his rescue.

And then Joe began to feel his own self bubbling with the assault on his dignity and on his body. As the pain of the two suspender snaps began to radiate across his chest, he got up and went to the bathroom, where he ministered to himself with a soothing cream that he ran lightly over the tread marks.

Tina stood at the kitchen end of the hall where the bathroom was situated. She knew that by placing herself in that spot she was creating a high noon of sorts. It might be here that they would have it out. The little place in her where dreams lived was hoping that he would hit her, not hard, but hard enough for her to declare that it was over between them without having to attend to all the drudge work that goes into a divorce: coldness ratcheting up; saying *No, thanks* to be spiteful when a *Yes* would be the considerate thing to do; dying to each other in the living room; watching the TV without commentary; reading alone in the bedroom; separation in the bed; the silences that speak indifference. The worst part was looking for a sign, any sign, that things could be different, that there might be a spark that she could again ignite the fire.

Tina wasn't sure if she wanted to go through that, though it was never the case in her that she doubted her own strength. With absolute conviction that came from the side room of consciousness, where only truth is allowed to be spoken, she knew that, when called upon, she had the courage of a lioness. Even as a teenager, buffeted about by other teens in her high school, she had an image in mind: if something she really wanted was on the other side of the room and she had to crawl naked over a floor cemented with pieces of sharp glass to get it, she would crawl, one knee at a time, and she would get it. Bloody knees, to be sure. But she would get it.

But doing the drudgework was different from a one-act drama, and she knew that. There was, though, one person whose happiness she was willing to work for. That was Christopher. For his sake, she would try to straighten this out. For him, she would be willing to crawl through the jagged glass. So, she turned around from the hallway and sat on a kitchen chair, acting as if nothing was wrong.

"Joe," she said, poking around for the tender spot where his need for the security of family lived, "there's a hockey game in town Thursday. I'd like you to take Christopher." She hesitated and then quickly backtracked. "What I mean is that you know how much he likes the game, and I thought it would be nice if you two could get out for a night together. I'll cook a steak for both of you so that as soon as you come home from the job, you can eat and get going."

He looked at her as if to say, "Tell me more," and they both breathed a sigh of relief to know that the battle would not be conjoined—on this day, at least.

"Sure," he said, "that'd be nice. We haven't done anything together in a long time."

Practically never, she said to herself. What she didn't know was that their outing to the hockey game might be the last thing Joe and Christopher ever did together.

15

By this time, Francis just knew it whenever Jesus wanted to see him. He didn't know how, but he knew. When Jesus would be sitting in the blue chair waiting for him to come home, he didn't get freaked out.

"Hi, Francis," he said in the kind of formal way he had at the beginning of each meeting. Francis thought he was shy. He was going to say *by nature,* but by now the business of the nature of Jesus was too confusing for him.

"Hello, Jesus," he answered, always in a very polite way.

In a solemn tone, Jesus gave a directive to him. "It's time for you to start the work. Please sit down."

Oh, man, he thought, *please let me out of here.* He was supposed to be starting a work, some work, *the* work. With Jesus, the son of God. He wanted to avoid it as much as possible, hoping that he would wake up from a dream, breathe a sigh of relief to know this was just a dream, and get on with his life, dull as he knew it was.

"From this moment on, your life will not be dull," he said. He stared at him, he thought, to see if he was all right. Sure enough.

"Are you okay, Francis?" he asked.

"Yes, I am. It's just that, well, you know that this is all like a dream to me. I mean, things like this just do not happen."

"I know. But the Father and I have confidence in you. In fact, we are offering you a gift of confidence. All you have to do is to say yes."

"Thank you. I accept," he said as fast as he could, because he knew that if he thought about it for a second more, he'd want to run. "Please, though, let me ask you, 'Why me?'"

"Why not you?" Jesus returned, adding, "This is not a rhetorical question."

It didn't take Francis long to answer him. "Because I'm not a good man, and I have lots of faults."

"Do you not know that I also have my faults? It is too bad that they wrote me up like I was perfect in every way. They did not see all the times when I suffered through my own expanding humanity. They did not know that I was once an adolescent who wasn't sure of himself and, in trying to find out who I was, discovered many of the same faults in me as you have." Then he asked him a question that seemed to tickle him.

"Do you want to know my biggest human defect, Francis?" He could only think of Mickey Mantle when he revealed publicly that he wet his pants at night into early adolescence. *Please, God, please don't make it anything like that.* "Well, yes, of course," he lied.

"I'm sorry. I'm just afraid of knowing these things. I don't know what you'll expect of me."

"In any case," he continued, "I'm going to tell you about my biggest defect, which I think is hilarious. It's that I'm so self-righteous. Remember I'm talking here as a man who took on the same humanity as you. I can be hurt by what you do, you know. The best part of the defect is that I can laugh about it. I think it's funny that I am so self-righteous. I like to think that I'm right about everything. Sometimes, it's about impossible for me to even imagine that the other person is right. I used to wonder if it was a trait that leaked out from my Godhead. I don't think so. I think that when my mother Mary agreed to bear me, I took on her genetic traits.

"I don't remember her trying to be right much of the time. But sometimes she was overbearing, especially when I was an adolescent. It was only later when I began to prepare for my mission that I knew she was right just about every time."

Jesus wanted to talk, and Francis was comforted to realize that he was relaxed with him.

"Why, I was so shy that I could barely look a girl in the face," he said. "I sometimes disobeyed my parents, did not always come home on time for the evening meal. I did draw the line at lying, though."

And then, in what he first thought was an irrelevant comment, he said, "I've noticed that you don't lie." He paused, a twinkle in his eye. "We'll give you a mulligan on the little white one you just told."

Francis was hoping he'd continue to digress from the business he had in mind. It was not to be.

"I think you are ready to hear what I have to say now, Francis. I know it is a lot. But we are confident that you can handle it. You have been chosen for this, let's call it a mission. I like the sound of that. You have been chosen," he repeated, "because you are a good man. You have slipped up now and then, you have treated your wife with less than the dignity and respect she deserves, and you have not always been present to your children. You are distant from your fellow workers, all good and decent people chosen to be in your life. You are responsible for these things, and we hope that some day you will make it up to them. Because you think of your defects mostly as omissions, you have excused yourself. Before we go on, remember that you are accountable for the things you do not do as well as the things you do."

What could he say? It wasn't as if this was some psychologist talking to him. "Thank you," is what he did say.

"I want to tell you why I have been visiting with you. You are a mailman and, as I've said, a good man. I didn't get that quite right. What I mean is that you are a good man *and* a mailman. The Father, who includes me, is tired, cosmically you might say, and I do not mean that as a joke. He is tired of people on Earth not progressing, not evolving, although I do not like to use that word, as people here make such a fuss over it.

He knows, of course, that the Great Flood was a traumatic time in the life of man. It was kind of normal at first for people to react to it with such selfishness. But then when the progressive overreaction continued, well here you are. I don't have to tell you about the last ninety years, as you count them and as you know them.

"I will just call it The Carnage, as the details of what you do to each other are almost too much for me to bear. The problem is that you lack faith. When I say *you,* I don't mean you, Francis Meeks. I mean the human race." Just as Francis was beginning to think he was an exception, Jesus said, "And, of course, you are a member and lack faith as much as any of them."

No matter what Jesus had just told him about being a good man, he could not account for the fact that he had chosen him out of the many. The fact was that he had, so he just accepted it without any more thinking about it. It just was.

"I will tell you, Francis, that you and the ones I will ask you to give letters to and speak with about me, doubt the intentions of the Father. You not only doubt, but also give up on ever knowing the answers to your questions about the ever-present and great concerns you have. Instead, you preoccupy yourselves with frivolous things. They are about bigness and whatness. How big is the thing and what can it do to make your life easier?

"The great questions are important because they really apply to each one of you. And because I am one of you, they apply to me also. You wonder about the

Father. Does he really exist? Where is he? What happens after we die? Is there a heaven, a hell? Where's Uncle John and Aunt May? And Fofinha, your little dog who was hit by a car when you were a small boy?" He paused before saying, "These are hard questions, and the Father has not made it easy to find the answers.

"So, most of you just give up and try to find the answers to trivial things. I know. I see you. And Council members tell me. You have settled for easy answers to small questions. You have settled only because the answers are obvious and after the fact, or you can figure them out with your minds. You cannot figure out the answers to the great questions that bother you all. And do you know why?"

Francis was overwhelmed, so he just sputtered out, "No, I don't," as fast as he could.

"Because you do not have faith that everything will be all right. Most humans have a little faith. They want to believe that things will be okay. But as soon as everything does not go their way, they stop believing. They stop experiencing the presence of the Father."

He felt like he was being reprimanded, and for a minute he forgot that he was talking to Jesus.

"But, where was the Father when the Holocaust was taking place? Why didn't he come down and strike the Nazi dead? He wasn't there; he seems to have gotten lost. Maybe he was indifferent, unreliable, insensitive." He was nearly shouting.

Jesus didn't seem to be upset. In fact, he seemed very calm. "Francis, why do you punish yourself so?"

He was about to ask him what he meant by that when he got back to the mail customers.

"I am going to expand the next day into what will seem like days to you. I am going to give you letters to deliver to Tina, Richard, William, Cora, and Nicholas. Except for William, who has a great-granddaughter who is Thomas's age, each of them has a child also about the same age as Thomas. Each of them plans to attend the Rangers' hockey game on Thursday. As I am also going to undo the physics of impenetrability, each of them might be sitting in the same seat at the same time. That is, they could occupy the same space."

"Jesus," I said, "this is getting weird."

"Only by your standards. It will get even weirder," he responded. "Each of the children, Christopher, Erin, Megan, Angelina, and Aaron, as well as your son Thomas, has the possibility of having something you think of as bad, and that I will call existential, happen to them on that day. It could happen to each one at the same time."

Of course, he asked him what was going to happen.

"You will know when it is time. For now, be certain that it will have something to do with a choice that you and each of the children's parents will make. Let us hope it is the right one."

16

RICHARD AND ERIN

Unit sixty-two, where Richard Darby lived with his daughter Erin, was the same size as the rest of the units in the apartment building where they lived. It only seemed smaller because of the amount of stuff strewn about all of its spaces, including drawers, shelves, and closets.

The disarray probably reflected Richard and Erin's inner life: they fit reality according to the lenses from which they viewed its possibilities. As you already know, Richard's lens had been distorted early on when his own drunken parents found amusement by hanging him out of their apartment window, first by two feet, then one.

So Richard became an alcoholic. He probably was one genetically, although the degree and consistency of his parents' drinking led him to believe that getting drunk often was normal. He was a boy of about eleven when his father first offered him a goblet of wine. For Richard, the drink gleamed like a large ruby encased in glass, with a hint of honeysuckle that made him giddy, a feeling he mistook for love. Thereafter, on each Thanksgiving, they offered a similar goblet to him, which made him drunk. Holding on to the walls of the hallway as he staggered toward his room was, for several years, the only remembrance of the holiday, now fuzzy and blurred.

Tired of his parents' sprees and their need to beat him about his legs and bloody his nose and ears with their drunken blows, Richard left home when he was seventeen to be a religious monk. He left also because he was ashamed that even as a teenager he often cried himself to sleep as he listened to them yell drunken obscenities at each other.

Somewhere deep inside him he wanted to love them. There was even a certain desperation about it as the desire progressed to a need. It was only much later that he realized that they were incapable of giving or receiving love, that he had to settle. In fact, a psychologist told him he would be served best if he simply considered them dead. He was grasping for anything, even band-aids at the time, and he took the advice and had little to do with them anymore.

Being a religious monk was nothing more than a welcomed distraction from the inner turmoil. The regularity and discipline of the life gave him a sense of order until the security of it all, day to day, wore off, leaving the emptiness in his psyche exposed once again. He was always too proud and ashamed to reveal his neediness, so he covered it by developing in himself what he thought of as an extreme case of holiness. He began to think of himself as the criterion for sainthood among his peers. In fact, his ways of acting and talking bore the marks of the fraud.

Once, for example, on a Friday night when a brother monk might volunteer to prostrate himself on the floor of the altar and confess a sinful breach against the community, Brother Richard practically threw himself down on the floor before humbly acknowledging that his turn at cooking that Wednesday had resulted in an inferior spaghetti sauce, one that ought not to have countenanced their approval, and would they, please, the next time that might happen, bring it to his attention. It was the epilogue that included the words *immediate* and *forthwith* that got their attention like a rolled-up three-dollar bill bouncing.

At about the same time as he was finding the life of a monk dissatisfying, he was discovering a loud voice in his loins that declared the existence of women. Although he had minimal contact, perhaps one or two stopping by to purchase a bottle of wine from the vineyard, it was enough to let him know that they existed. He wanted them, all of them, he thought.

Before he left the monks, though, his superior told him that he was like a rubber band stretched to the max; just a bit more and it might snap.

If Richard was a genetic alcoholic, he was also one by temperament. Fear was easily sparked in him. He dreaded to walk the dark stairs of the apartment building where he grew up, because he always expected that a boogeyman would jump out at him from the shadows. He was afraid of dogs, and whenever a car backfired, he would feel an electric shock run through him from head to toe. He learned to be careful when carrying a drink, something he would later often do. Once, at a friend's house, he sprayed a gin and tonic all over the living room couch when his friend surprised him from behind with a manly greeting, a smack on the back.

He might have been alive to the fear and dread he carried around, might have known that the drama he always felt in his body, the fast inner clock, was a disorder from the childhood abuse heaped upon him if his stress disorder had only been given a name outside those victimized by war. As it was, he hid from himself by trying to cultivate a life of prayer as a monk and later by attempting to self-medicate with alcohol. Mostly, though, neither one of these slowed things down. He only pretended they did.

The prayer life, artificially developed as it was according to certain formulas, became a veneer of holiness beneath which the bugs of anxiety continued to crawl. The only way he could stop them from eating at his stomach was to lie on his bed, face down, and then get up on all fours. The worms rested as long as he remained in that position with his stomach hanging down. He could feel them again as soon as he stood up.

More than anything, it was the worms. His talents as an accountant, though sufficient, were never enough to get him past the junior status. His daily drinking began to affect his work. Getting the numbers wrong or turning them in late would not cut it, and he lost jobs. Although he always managed to get work, it was usually on a part-time basis. During the in-between stretches, his relationship with his wife, Shelley, and his child began to erode in an almost organic, progressive, and predictable way. Time under the influence begged him to find others wrong, including those to whom he owed money.

When on a drunken spree, he loved to tell friends, with great justification, how it was a God-given right for his house to be heated and for him to communicate with others on the telephone, all for free. For these rights, he would always use the word *inalienable*. He thought the word brought an intellectual, philosophical, and historical context to his argument. Needless to say, his bill of debtor rights cut him little slack. Each time the electricity or the telephone service was cut off, he would drink more. Shelley got more angry, and Erin more confused. Soon, Shelley and Erin began to withdraw from Richard, to a safer place, they thought. Left alone much of the time, Richard began to live in his head and soon discovered that this was a dangerous place to hang out alone.

His drinking increased and his conduct became more and more shadowy, as he often retreated into the room he liked to call his "study." There, he could take refuge in thinking and in the bottles of liquor hidden under the big armchair and in the closet between folded clothes on the top shelf. He would sit in the armchair, pretending to read (just in case Shelley took him by surprise) and nurturing thoughts about life's unfairness and how others were responsible for his lack of progress as an accountant. That if his bosses could only see the depth of his talents, he would soon become one of them. He would think about how Shelley did not understand him, that his directions about family matters were based on the solid experience and wisdom that she did not have. And he wondered endlessly why Erin did not want to spend time with him, never getting it that he did not make sense to her, much less anyone else, in the always groggy and silly ways that he articulated himself.

He did not realize that his drunken ways were exacerbating the natural difficulty children often have in accepting what they see as the weirdness of parents. She did not want to be around him, nor would she ever ask her friends to come into her parents' apartment again after her tenth birthday party, when Richard came home from work early as a surprise. What he did that day became the straw that broke the camel's back of her dutiful attempts to love him. He thought it was very funny when he took the vanilla cream cake her mother baked especially for the party and, in front of Erin's friends, stuffed it into her face as if he was at some kind of frat party. He thought it was so funny that he nearly cried. For Erin, it was so sad that she did cry.

He didn't understand the lack of humor in Shelley's tone that night when she tried to explain why Erin probably would not want to show her face at school for a couple of hundred years. The more he got drunk, the less he was able to understand what was normal.

Yet, he tried, and in the attempt, caused the death of his wife. He told Shelley that he would stop drinking, and he apologized to his daughter. He told her that her peers would forget her silly old man in time and she should get on with the business of having fun while growing up.

Richard did not drink for two weeks before the accident. He even tried to convince Shelley of his goodwill by putting out the garbage and doing the dishes after dinner. He stopped going to his study and spent a little time each night with his wife and daughter, "the girls," as he renamed them during this sober period. He would take great delight after doing the dishes in asking them to sit with him for a minute before inviting them to answer the question, "What would *the girls* like to do tonight?" By his edict, the choices were *Monopoly* on nights that Erin wanted to be a part of the family or checkers with Shelley. As she was much better at this than he, the activity was changed to seven-card stud poker, a card game he invented to most nearly match his skills at sequencing sets and matching numbers.

There was a new spirit in the house, and who knows? It might have gone far toward restoring harmony to the family. Along with it, though, came spontaneity, an undisciplined part of Richard's psychic anatomy that sometimes led him into trouble.

On the afternoon of the Saturday when they had accepted an invitation to dinner at a friend's apartment, Shelley decided that she wanted a new dress for the evening. She was excited, as this would be the first time in a long while that she and Richard had accepted an invitation out. When he was with friends for dinner, as compared to parties where he thought there was automatic license to get drunk, he managed to hide many of the contrary ways that might follow the third or fourth drink. But Shelley remembered the exceptions and so was reluctant to go anywhere with him. Though, with a few weeks of sobriety under his belt, she thought, the night would be safe enough.

"Richard, I'm going to buzz over to the mall to get a dress for tonight," she told him as a matter of fact. It felt good to be like this, she thought, after all the years of calculating how she could tell him about going to the store or to lunch with a girlfriend without exciting an easily provoked jealousy or a feeling of anger because he thought she was rejecting his company.

A lurking tad of generosity suddenly poked its head through the layers of crust, and he volunteered to drive her there. She wasn't used to this kind of attention, declined his offer, and began to collect whatever it was that she needed for the purchase, excited and happy that a predictable Richard would be there when she came home.

Then she saw the look on his face, the puppy-dog look. "Okay," she said, "why don't you take me there? We can have a little fun picking out the dress."

Shelley was so excited to be with him that she felt the glow of happy dating days. She tried on several dresses, each time coming out of the dressing room like she was a runway model, strutting exaggerated cross-over strides, posing first with the right hip out, then the left. Each time, he'd laugh and she'd giggle. They settled on a kind of baby-girl dress, young in its design, but just right for the night.

And then it happened. They were waiting at the light to pull out of the mall parking lot. When the light changed, Richard, with the residue of irritability left by alcohol leaving his body, made a quick left-hand turn. The screeching of brakes, the metallic sounds of a small truck crashing into Shelley's side, and the gasps and gurgles came as a surprise to Richard. He simply did not see the drunken truck driver run the light. The coroner told him later that if only the truck was smaller or larger, if only its grill was higher or lower, it would not have smacked her so bluntly on the face and neck.

By the time a neighbor brought young Erin to the hospital, her mother was dead. Since she was used to knee-jerking blame on her father, she would not talk to him for a long time after the tragedy. It was, too, a way for her to punish him for all the wrongs she had seen him inflict upon her mother over the years.

17

BILL AND MEGAN

It's not so tough to imagine that an eighty-seven-year-old guy like Bill could love his great-granddaughter as much as he loved little Megan. She was, as it is said, the apple of his eye. To give you an idea: once when she was about five, Bill came to pick her up from nursery school. Miss Chatterton, her teacher, met him at the door with a sort of breathless gasp.

"I am so glad you are here, Mr. Waxman. All I've heard for the past two hours is 'Grandpa Bill is coming today. Grandpa Bill is coming today.'"

And when Megan, coiled energy waiting to be released, was set free by Miss Chatterton, she sprang from the back of the room into Bill's arms with such force that she knocked him on his back. In the loving tumble of generations, Bill broke his arm. Needless to say, Megan was inconsolable for the damage she had done to her beloved granddad. She only stopped crying when, after the emergency clinic folks doctored Bill's arm and put it in a sling, he took her to one of the small toyshops in Shrewsbury and just about begged her to get whatever she wanted. Having her own Lincoln Logs did the trick.

In-between and during the work of their new-found logging company, which Bill called "The Bill-megans," later changed by the apple to "The Megan-bills," she smothered his face with so many kisses that afternoon that Bill didn't shave the next morning. He told his own daughter, Suz, on the phone the next day that he didn't have to; that nothing could grow under the onslaught of all those kisses. She knew better, that he probably hadn't yet washed off any of them from his face.

Bill had much to bring to the table of life, maybe because he had killed so many men early on. The senselessness of it all gave him, in retrospect, an appreciation for the delicacy of things. Mostly, though, his experiences taught him how easy it is to have life taken away.

He did most of his killing in the Northern Marianas islands during WWII. He had joined the marines in early 1942, soon after Pearl Harbor. Like so many young men of his generation, he thought it a privilege to fight for his country. If any single interpretation of his attitude during the period of his training were to be made, it might be summed up as being "jacked." His father used to tell his neighbors that the war would be over in about sixty days if all the young men being prepared to fight were as enthusiastic as

Bill about the killing. Bill would tell his parents in his letters that, "The Japs are bad guys, really bad guys. We are told that they will do anything to kill as many of us before they die as they can. They are ruthless. They are like animals, not fully human."

And in blood-curdling predictions, he would tell his parents, "I will kill as many of them as I can, no matter what." Such was their own disposition about the enemy that it was only the *no matter what* part that bothered them.

Well, he did get the chance. He learned to enhance his hatred; not, though, in small doses. The first time he saw the mutilated bodies of fellow marines, he made a quantum leap from the idea of killing, to killing with gusto and glee. Although some of his buddies were involved in hand-to-hand combat with the enemy, he killed at first from a distance, picking off a few from fifty yards or so. This did not then bother him.

What did bother him near the end of the battle on Saipan was watching the native Chamorro women jump off the cliffs. "Suicide Cliffs," the Marines called it, at Marpi Point in the north. The Japanese had told the locals that if they surrendered, the Americans would rape their women, boil their children, and subjugate their men.

For hours, Bill and other Marines stood helplessly, watching women throw their babies off the 800-foot drop onto the jagged rocks below before hurling themselves to what Bill hoped was a better place. It was mostly, though, the tenderness that many of the women expressed as they jumped together with

their children that moved Bill to an ever-greater commitment to keep his unwanted promise to his own
parents. He watched these women wrap their arms
around a tiny baby—a few times he saw two babies,
one in each arm—and pull the child into their stomach, a treasure protected, or so they wished, before
hunkering down into a fetal position and pushing off
into the unknown.

Each time that Bill or one of the other marines
tried to go among them to stop the madness, an
enemy soldier among the confused and desperate people would shoot at them, or a sniper in a rocky cave
would fire. He didn't know why, yet every time one of
the native men jumped off the cliffs, he did it with his
back to the sea.

The indelible mark left by this experience would
show up in Bill now and then, but mostly as he got
older. Sometimes a certain kind of music would get
him to thinking about those babies. He allowed the
tears to run down his face, but only when he was
alone. Though, sometimes he couldn't hold them back
when he was with Megan.

"Why are you crying, Grandpa Bill?" she'd ask.
Mostly, he'd find an excuse, like the wind blowing, or
the sun in his eyes. Once, when it happened indoors,
he said that an air-conditioner could sometimes do
that to his eyes. Sometime along the way, she stopped
believing him when this happened. She would then
hug him tightly in the way that little girls can, until
she knew he was ready to resume his usual ways. Bill

would wipe his eyes and wait for the pain of holding back the lump in his throat to subside.

He was in his 70s when he began to question what he had done on the island of Iwo Jima in 1945. There was his wife, Jane; the two kids, Suz and David; and his always-growing orthopedic business (each of these and the busy-ness that goes with tending) that kept his mind pinned to practical matters for the greater part of his life.

It was Jane's death from a lingering heart problem that taught him to go beyond tending and toward deep loving. Near her end, after all that could be done was done, he began to feel something different inside himself. He always knew that he loved her, and he could still, after all these years, call up the way he felt when he first saw her, dancing alone one late evening on a powdery sand beach on the north shore of Long Island. She had on a summer dress that he swore was worn-out from looking good. She was spinning in slow-motion softness before she became aware of the stolen looks that he was taking. Pretending not to see him, she continued while he became puffed out and giddy as a kid. She could tell. And he could tell. When this happened, he thought that her spirit was in her hips, which became like a wiggling top, spinning endlessly. Immediately, he was in awe of her and began to know the thrill of falling in love: feeling the joy, dreading the pain.

During the last months of her lingering illness, something inside him that he had mostly smothered since the days when he joyfully killed enemy soldiers began to surface to take on an authenticity he had never known. Without a doubt, Bill knew it had started with his long-time buddy, a beagle he named Roxie that he had picked up off the streets after he was released from his pledge to kill Japs. No matter his irritability, which was considerable after he came back, the dog was always there for him. Even when he tried to shush her away, she would lick his face and wag her tail, as if she couldn't help it.

Looking back, Bill realized that it was his first taste of love without reservation, something he admitted to no one until one day near the end of Jane's last stay in the hospital when he told her. "How simple," he said, as they waited in her room for her to be unloosed from technology and turned over exclusively to Bill's loving care. How simple that a need to express his love for her and the ache he was feeling for her now started long ago with a tiny beagle called Roxie.

It wasn't as if he hadn't always loved her, he explained to Jane. He told her how from the first moment he saw her on the beach that he knew. And then he asked her forgiveness for the times that he knew it, felt it, and did not express it. He just didn't always know how, he told her.

The seasons between killing on Iwo Jima and revealing his heart to Jane that day were sometimes filled with nightmares about what he had done and despair that he would never be able to let her know the depths of what she meant to him. It was as if the power of the training to be a soldier had put a wrap over his spirit. Some nights, the fears and despairs mingled in his dreams. He would see Jane on a beach of volcanic black sand, sinking into the softness of it, all while enemy soldiers stuck bayonets into her chest. Half asleep, he could never stop them. He would sit up in bed and in a low timbre blow out an animal noise through tight lips before his own increasingly loud moans woke him up. After a few times, Jane got used to his fears fluttering in the night and would calmly soothe him back to sleep. "It's all right, baby, it's all right," she would coo over and over until he fell asleep again.

When Jane died, he not only lost his best friend of sixty years, but also the only one he ever fully trusted. His natural tendency to be trusting tried to surface every now and then during his early years, but it was easily hammered down by his experiences, especially the magnitude of what he had done on the tiny island.

Although he saw only one soldier above ground (a man he stumbled upon before shooting him in the chest) during the thirty-three days he spent on the small island, he killed, by his own count, about forty Japanese soldiers. He was one of the young marines whose contempt for death lead them into many of the caves on the island with a certainty that they would not be killed. At first, he liked to tell his buddies that they were "mercy killings," the *coup de grace* administered to soldiers who had mangled themselves with hand grenades, yet not sufficiently enough to die for their Emperor, a service he gave at the time with a sneer and a joyful contempt that would later haunt him.

He might have, if it were not for Jane, become one of the ones whose manhood is sucked dry by the orgy of killing. The nightmares kept her on guard, and whenever she got an inkling that his spirit was being pulled into the past, she intervened. She would simply increase the intensity of her constant love. If it was usually at a nine, she would, at those times, bump it up to a ten by wrapping her warmth around the fragility of his growing awareness that what he had done as a young man he now found despicable. That was something that he could not undo, awake or in his asleep.

He could not get those forty men out of his mind. It would get worse if the remorse came upon him when Megan was around. Some of them might have had a Noriyo, a Yushimi, a Megan of their own, that is, if he hadn't killed them. He often wondered now how he could have thought of them as monkeys, now when his respect for living things had grown so much that he wouldn't even kill a fly.

One early morning, Jane found him kneeling next to his bed in what seemed like prayer. He was embarrassed. *Not manly,* he thought. "I was talking to the men I killed," he told her. As he rarely spoke about the war, it was news to her that he had killed anyone, though a smart lady like her suspected as much might be true.

"Would you like to tell me about it?" she asked, realizing at once that she had struck the lodestone which pulled him to the increasing days of sitting in his study chair and staring ahead, almost as if he was watching a secret movie on the wall at the other end of the room.

He got out the part about how he had been asking them for forgiveness, but when he started to tell her that they never spoke back to him, he cried so hard that she was afraid his chest and shoulders might disengage from the rest of his body or that the tear ducts of his eyes might never work again. Such was the flow that washed his face, and, she hoped, his soul.

"Dear Bill, my dear, dear Bill," she said as she held him to herself, "have you asked God to forgive you?" She knew him, and she knew that to keep a moment like this intact, it must be kept simple. This was not the time to remind him about how young he was then, that the country was at war with a fanatical enemy, that kind of stuff. Time had reduced considerations such as these to an irrelevant smallness for him.

"I have," he responded as he tried to regain himself. "But, he never answers me. 'Please, God,' I say, 'please forgive me.'" The old prescriptions about men not crying took hold, and he did not want to cry again. Instead, he laughed a small laugh, the kind that said he was bewildered about what he couldn't verbalize.

"Did I ever tell you about the time I was alone in our backyard," Jane said, "needing forgiveness so bad for something I had said to Suz, stubborn Suz? She was a little girl at the time, but she wouldn't accept my apology. Just stood her ground to make me sweat. Anyway, while I sat in the yard, a big mother crow landed nearby, and I thought she looked at me. 'Mrs. Crow,' I said to her, 'I screamed at my daughter today.

I'm sorry but she won't forgive me, and I don't know what to do.' I began to think about how silly I would look if one of the neighbors caught a glimpse of me talking to a bird about our little girl when it suddenly dawned on me what to do.

"'Mrs. Crow, I'm sorry I was so cross with my girl today, and I'm sorry that she won't forgive me.' I paused, and the crow was still. 'Will you forgive me, Mrs. Crow?' I asked. I've always felt kind of silly about this, Bill, so I've never told you how she looked up at me and then walked away bobbing her head as if to say, 'Well yes, of course I will.'"

"You never told me," he said, his heart swollen by her goodness right then.

"You know, if God doesn't answer you, well, maybe it's for a reason. Maybe he wants you to forgive yourself first. Maybe then he'll answer you."

With all their other distractions, they had never shared the depths of their prayer life with each other. What she said then came as a surprise. "Bill, maybe you can start by your asking *me* to forgive you?" she said, more like an answer than a question. "If God does not speak to you now, maybe you can try me."

The tough, practical part of Bill sometimes took over at the wrong time, rendering his most loving motives useless.

"But you'd always forgive me, no matter what," he said. She gave him a look whose nuances only he could interpret. The way her lip and cheeks connected at times like this reminded him of the way his mother looked at him when something he did or said as a child annoyed her.

"Don't bet on it, Buster," Jane said to him.

They laughed, and then she heard his confession. His tears were few. Perhaps the pain had already begun to shake itself out through his chest and shoulders. Then Jane gave him absolution by holding his face in her hands and looking him in his eyes before saying, "In the name of God, I forgive you, William Waxman. Now please forgive yourself."

Maybe it was the regard and respect he had for her, maybe it was God's presence in the room, or that he was working through this extraordinary woman. Whatever it was, Bill knew that right then, without any words spoken, that he had been forgiven.

Of course, when Jane died, there was a hole in Bill's heart about the size of the Grand Canyon. He really didn't want to live without her. There wasn't any point to it anymore. Suz tried hard to enkindle in him a spark. She came to his house often, brought him meals, even got him a ticket for a cruise to the Antarctic, hoping it would break him out of the despair he felt.

Megan's mom, Kathrine, a single mother more intent on her career as a professor of anthropology than on spending much time with Megan, thought it wonderful how little Megan and her great-granddad hit it off, though she didn't know that Megan was what stood between Bill's will to live and cutting the umbilical to life.

Bill wasn't quite sure why he was so taken with

Megan. At first he thought it was that he could see some of his beloved Jane in her face. Then he started to notice that the more time he spent with her, the more the Grand Canyon began to shrink. He could find Jane's innocence and simplicity in her way of seeing things. There were times when Bill wanted to correct this in her, but then he'd think of where these ways got Jane to some wonderful place that he thought no one else could ever go. When he noticed that Megan was heading in the same direction as Jane, he didn't even try to remind her that Tommy, the class bully according to the way Bill saw things, was not just "having a bad day, Grandpa," when he took Megan's candy bar, but that he was being a bad kid. Then he thought of Jane and how she would have put it—"good kid, bad deed"—a little surprised that Megan hadn't said it just that way.

Maybe it was simply that she was an extremely good person, the likes of which he had known only in Jane. It wasn't that he didn't look for this in others. It was just that in the desperate attempt to find some goodness in himself after the killings, he had unknowingly become a hunter, with himself the prey. When he realized that he didn't even know what he was looking for, he set the standards for others so high that only Jane could reach them. And now that she was gone, only Megan could.

It was sometimes sad for him to babysit Megan when her mom was on one of the many busy spells that began to define her life, especially the times when Megan would tell him about how much she missed her mom, and how she, even now as a little girl, wanted to become a nurse so she could help others. Now and then, she would confide in Bill that she'd like to take the place of some invalid girl her age she might see at the mall. Whenever she said things like that, Bill rediscovered whatever residual hope he had, just by looking at her face, where he would find the template for goodness.

Except for the occasional juicy steak and fried onions that involuntarily thrilled his taste buds, being with Megan was his single pleasure in life. It was, then, not a surprise to Suz and Kathrine the day when he announced to them that he and the girl would be going ice-skating at the local lake on Saturday. "I'm surprised you did not know," he told Kathrine with a tad of pique in his tone, "that your daughter wants to learn how to ice-skate." Such was his hold on Megan's affections and her mother's reliance on his willingness to watch over the girl that she didn't smack a hardball return.

"No, I didn't," was all she said.

"Did she tell you that I bought us ice skates?"

"No," she answered, making sure that this simple word was not charged with the anger she was beginning to feel.

The ice-skating adventure was, by any measure, a success. Bill managed to get his skates on properly and only twice bruised his butt. Of course, when he fell just about everyone came to his rescue. Old man down will do that. As for Megan, she managed to skate shaky circles in a counter-clockwise motion. She seemed to like going in that direction.

An hour or so was enough before hot chocolate at the diner, where Bill asked Megan how she liked ice-skating. Her enthusiastic and giggly response prompted him to ask her if she would like to see the Rangers game at the Garden. There, he told her, is where she could see strong men turn the wobbly edges she had barely managed at the pond that morning into swift, clean, and graceful lines.

"Like I draw lines on the computer?" she asked.

"Yes, just like that," he said, not yet knowing that what might happen at the hockey game would happen "just like that."

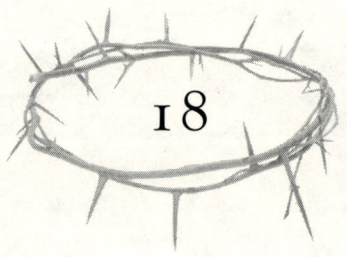

18

CORA AND ANGELINA

Cora was not an ordinary slut. Fact is, she wasn't a high-class one either, though she liked to think of herself as superior. When she first started to cheat on Bob, her husband of twelve years, she was very careful to drive across the Throgs Neck Bridge, get onto I-95 into Connecticut, and then off, in the beginning at Stamford, later in Greenwich, where she thought the bars had more quality. Where they were moody with undertones in the music and nuances in the shades of light, which she thought of as *darklight*. Sometimes, when she was testing new bars for new men, if she wasn't sure if there was darklight, she would pretend to look for someone so she could leave without having to buy the first drink. An unaccompanied woman as pretty as she would be hit on quickly, so she knew that if she didn't want to stay, a first drink was one drink too many.

It was the darklight that fed her romantic long-ings, forgotten by Bob since she got the nose job that angered him. Cora's nose was slightly tilted so that from a certain angle it had a ski-lift kind of look. When Bob was still romantic with her, he would comment on her face—forehead, eyes, cheek bones, chin, nose—every part of her beautiful face, always reminding her that it was her nose, the brushstroke that brought it all together, that gave beauty to the piece. In his awkward way with words, he would tell her that her nose was "the catalyst" that changed the ordinary into the extraordinary.

One of life's mysteries for Bob was why she had her nose fixed. She was careful not to have the slope made straight as an arrow, just had it unbowed a bit. But it was enough to drive Bob away from her, his ego hurt badly by the rebuttal of what defined beauty for him.

After letting the pressure of not venting his anger build to the point of eruption, he decided to mind his temper and confront her in the best way he could, a way he knew her more schooled self might appreciate.

"Would an artist change the Mona Lisa look?" he asked her, being careful to let slip the word *change* as softly as he could. "Would an architect alter the face of the Statue of Liberty just because it looked like Elvis Presley?" he said, trying to allude to her nose.

"No, he wouldn't," he answered his own questions. Before she had a chance to respond, he summoned up the saddest tone of voice he could before murmuring, "I loved your nose."

In the months that Bob began to grow away from

her, she missed the trips to the clubs where they usually joined his friends in the city fire department. As it turned out, these were the salad days for her. They had a great babysitter for Angelina, she was making money as a medical office manager, and he was doing fine as a fireman.

Cora did love the parties, the drinking, the innocent flirtations, enough to let her know how attractive she was to men, made easier because Bob didn't seem to care. He didn't notice that she was a moth drawn to fire.

At first, she tried to resist the rugged, flirtatious ways of Bob's buddies. She even found it cute when one of them pounded drunkenly on the locked bathroom door one night, trying to get her to come out so he could dance with her again.

She and Bob never talked about his withdrawal, which in time became mutual. Parties became her testing grounds for the viability of a double life. Before this, she didn't take much notice of the agreed-to manipulations that were taking place at the parties. When one of the men drove a friend's drunken wife home without her husband, who stayed behind to comfort the driver's wife (a cat lover whose kitty had been recently killed by a car), Cora thought it a show of generosity all around. And when one of her girlfriends danced into a bedroom with another's husband, she pretended not to notice. That is, until the other husband was Bob.

Although she said nothing to him about the betrayal, it served as a permission slip for her to accept more fully the advances made toward her. Soon, word got around that Cora was ready for the taking. When that happened, she began to dress more provocatively for the get-togethers: dresses higher from the bottom, lower from the top. She even found herself panting now and then at the advances of a particularly attractive man, and wished that she might tell him to explore further down her back or along her thigh. When the urge grew stronger, she danced closer, an open invitation for exploration and conquest.

Unwittingly at first, Cora continued to polish her technique. As she grew bolder about her needs for affection, Bob began to follow his own path. His drinking and carousing fit the pattern of someone trapped inside an ego only bruised, but not yet bloodied. It was the craziness that made his friends and Cora take notice, they by the brotherhood, she by the tiny residue of concern left from years of living together.

It was brought to the attention of his supervisors that he began to get manic when the alarm bell rang, a signal that roused the men to a serious pursuit of excellence. At those times, Bob would whoop and holler like a Hollywood Indian while he got ready. At first, the men took it as an attempt to lighten things up before they sensed that something might be wrong with him.

One afternoon, in the middle of an apartment fire, Bob discovered a piano in one of the units on fire and sat down to play, an odd thing in itself. It was that he chose "Smoke Gets in Your Eyes" to serenade the men fighting the fire that the benefit of doubt wrought by witnessing a marriage on the rocks was now rendered inapplicable. He was dropped from their sympathies.

At about the same time as Cora felt ready to venture beyond the parties and wander up the coastline of Connecticut, Angelina, who truly was a little angel, began to notice that all was not right with her parents. She watched as they ate dinner together without speaking and wondered why. She listened as they spoke words that barely hid the loathing they had for each other, and she knew that things were terribly wrong between them. She wondered why he began to come home late at night.

Whenever she asked her mother about this, Cora offered her lollipops. "Your father is just tired from working such long hours and needs to get out of the house," forgetting that Angelina might also question the time he spent at home with his best friends, a can of beer and a game (any game) on the TV.

In time, the logic of her Catholic upbringing supported Cora's decision to see other men. If thinking about being in bed with other men would bring her eternal damnation, as she was taught, she might as well have the fun of doing it.

As soon as she reached a settlement with the moral imperatives that ran her life, she began to work up the resolve to search for darklight. As Bob's indifference precluded any questions about her whereabouts, she was interrogated about "working overtime" and "seeing my girlfriends over the bridge" by Angelina, and that only by inference. "You weren't here to say good-night to me," or "How come we don't eat at six o'clock every night, the way we used to?"

At first, Cora's absences were sporadic, as she had only so much willingness to search for the right bars. Fear stalked her at every turn. The way men nursing drinks at a bar would turn, as if puppets on a common string, to look at her as she walked in made her turn red. After a while, though, she began to accept that she might have whichever one of them she wanted. That, too, took some getting used to.

In the beginning, she would sit, order a drink, and wait for a man's advances, though she learned in time that there was little correlation between boldness and appeal. For weeks she bluffed her way through, not really knowing what to do. With the considerable skills she had learned as an office manager, she would prattle on until the man lost interest or got up and left, once he concluded that verbiage was not what he was after.

The struggles eventually became part of her bag of tricks. She learned how, if she didn't want to accept an overture, she could repulse it by sharing an imaginative dark side. If she followed, "I felt like blowing his head off," with a cutie-pie question like, "Would you like me to blow your head off?" the pickup artist might begin to take one of his legs off the bar stool rest. And when she learned the nuances of a remark like this and caught the right tone to go with the man of her choice, she learned how to turn dross into gold.

All the while through the learning curve of pick-up management, she watched how other women handled themselves. How they left an unwanted partner with simple remarks like, "I must go now; it has been nice talking to you." She noticed that it was done quickly, before the guy had a chance to ask for her number or offer his card. She noticed, too, that once a man had been rejected by a woman that she did not stick around to continue playing this game that might easily spark jealousy in a lonely man once rejected by her.

The hardest part was learning when to stop drinking and to conduct her affairs in the four hours total time (including driving) she allotted to the activity. If she drank too much, she knew from experience that she could lose her ability to discriminate. What she did not want was to wake up in bed with the kind of man her sober sensibilities might not accept. As far as she could figure, this meant bad breath and a hairy chest. Doing an overnight would probably bring about the end of her marriage, as she was not talented at creating a big lie. Trying to explain her absence for a whole night might precipitate a string of jealous questions from Bob, questions that would force them both to face reality, something she did not want to do right now, mostly for Angelina's sake.

She was, then, very careful about how much she drank and what kind of man she took to bed, usually in a first-class motel or hotel in the area. Occasionally, one of the men she allowed to pick her up lived alone in a place nearby, where they would go, though never twice. Cora did not want her face to be known, something she thought could happen if she were seen twice.

In time, though, she developed a network of bars,

visiting each in a cycle which usually took about two months to complete. In this way, she hoped that she would not gather a reputation as an easy woman, nor would the same men always be there.

It was only after the excitement of this deceitful adventure wore off that Cora began to have second thoughts, which did not make her stop. As hard as she tried to understand her behavior, she could not. It was as if there was something drawing her to it that was more baffling and powerful than she. If there was any spark of fidelity left in Cora during this period of her life, it was to Angelina.

Angelina's birth was a dream come true. When the nurse placed her little swaddle-wrapped body into Cora's arms, she seemed to glow. It was as if her eyes absorbed her mother's loving gaze before reflecting it back with the same intensity as it was given.

The goodness that prevailed in man before the disobedience seemed to live in the baby. She was, indeed, a package of beautifully wrapped gifts that appeared to be sent to earth by God himself: twinkling eyes, laughter triggered by mom or dad's funny face, a button nose, nimble fingers that liked to grab *just because*.

It was the constancy of goodness that made her different. She could not stand cruelty. One day when she was five, she cried when one of the neighbors crushed the long-hated domestic cockroach beneath his boot. And when the older boys on a summer's evening trapped fireflies in their mothers' leftover mayonnaise jars, she would try to set them free.

Whenever she got into trouble at school, it was

usually for slapping down, or at least trying to, one of the bully boys for hurting another child. She was suspended in eighth grade because she would not be a part of the vivisection of frogs. Now and then, she would interrupt a teacher's lecture by boldly leaving her seat to scoop up a ladybug trying to make its long and slow journey from one side of the classroom to the other. As a nun reprimanded her for the interruption, Angelina would calmly place the bug in one of the plants that lined the old wooden windowsill. "We don't want her to get crushed, now do we?" she would ask, sweetly enough to end the episode.

Looking back, it was not hard for Cora to understand these ways of her daughter. After all, even though she got her nosed fixed, she, too, was a good person, loving her husband and daughter as much as any woman in the apartment house could love theirs. But as Bob's aloofness from her grew and she assumed a wayward behavior, her feelings for Angelina also grew, ironically, with some sad consequences.

She began to attach her unattended needs to be loved to her daughter. She became a friend rather than a mother. When Angelina would come home late from an afternoon at her girlfriend's apartment, Cora reminisced with her about how hard it was for her, too, to get home in time for dinner when she was a girl that age. And when her grades began to fall, it was easier to sympathize than to encourage. In time, she allowed a frightened Angelina to sleep in bed next to her. While trying to coo her to sleep, she would ask Angelina, in an attempt to ingratiate herself, where she would most in life like to go. "Anywhere out of here," she always answered.

"Too vague," she was told. "Be specific."

"Okay, take me to a hockey game," she retorted, before adding, "I mean it, Mom. I like hockey. I've been watching it lately on TV when you come home late. I like it. I like the way they glide. It seems like an easy way to float around your world." Her romantically sweeping ways of talking did not surprise Cora, as she was more and more expressing herself that way.

Allowing her child to sleep in bed with her became a sort of mini-shock that jolted Cora back into the reality that she was a mother and still a wife. She began to realize that the only part of her infidelities that continued to have any excitement for her was the chase. Her hobby of looking at a line-up of men in a magazine to decide which one she would like to take to bed had grown from fantasy to a kind of actuality. The spark to sex, though, began to wane. Once the flirtations moved on to the bed, she was no longer interested. Sometimes, she would tolerate the act while looking at the ceiling, praying for it to end quickly. When it ended, she would dress quickly before saying goodbye in a kind of "see you around" sort of way.

She tried to make a few overtures to Bob, but they were not well received. He had embarked on his own path and was enjoying it so much that he didn't even care that his ways had become scandalous. In fact, he turned indifference into asset, as women inclined to roam began to seek him out.

One night, after Angelina had gone to sleep, Cora

confronted him. She could not, though, dent the wall of apathy he had erected. He had a remarkable ability to box off the implications of his behavior, so that he was living the life of an active bachelor without any self-recrimination. On this night, Angelina became the trump card in their game.

"You don't even talk to your daughter any more," she suddenly yelled at him.

"Why should I?" he said. "She doesn't talk to me."

The exasperation of the past few months began to surface. "Don't you even know any more the difference between being a grown-up and a child?"

Perhaps his mind was triggered by the last heard reference. While pursing his lips, he answered, "I'm just a widdle boy and don't know better."

Cora had tried a straight shot to where she thought he might still tick. She was quick to realize that he didn't tick there anymore; that she was married to a stranger who was, perhaps, just a little boy.

"Your daughter likes hockey," Cora blurted out in a recriminating tone.

"The price of apples has gone up in Newfoundland," he said back.

With the strength of a woman who will not allow her spirit to be entirely sucked into the emptiness of another, she told him that she would do it herself, that he might as well disappear again this coming Thursday night, because she and Angelina would be going to see the Rangers game at the Garden.

19

NICHOLAS AND BEVERLEY

Nicholas and Beverley were no longer married when Jesus decided to visit Francis. Nicholas had broken off the marriage several years before, telling his wife that he feared for her emotional welfare if they were to stay together. He explained to her one August afternoon that he was drifting toward insanity. Since he cared for her so much, a divorce was the best way for her to not get hurt when he arrived at his presumed destination.

Of course, she was shocked when it happened. They had what is considered a good marriage. He was a banker, she an office manager. Together they made enough to provide for their two children, Aaron, ten, and Lisa, eight, who were both doing well in school and had no obvious problems. No ADD, OC disorders, no psychic boils about to erupt. They seemed well adjusted, having a normal number of disagree-

ments over territory, the average number of verbal
spats. They more or less did as they were told by
Nicholas and Beverley, and kept most of the house-
hold rules, the exception being the boy's preoccupation with watching hockey games on TV. Although at
first they didn't think it was good for him to spend his
Saturday afternoons and several evenings during the
week in front of the TV set watching the games, they
eventually gave in, reinforcing each other's parental
pride in their son's articulation of the game as a metaphor for life. There was the give and take, the bumps
and bruises, the ups and downs, the quick blending
of offense and defense, the quest toward the achieve-
ment of a goal. It was well-thought-out bullshit by
the boy whose cleverness with words never ceased to
amaze his parents.

It was Nicholas's motives in breaking up with his
wife that upset Jesus, who saw in him the typical and
ever-more-frequent occurrence of a failure to have
faith. He no longer believed that his needs as a growing man could be met by Beverly; no longer believed
in the possibilities of life, the very life given to him by
the Father.

By the third year of their marriage, Nicholas was
convinced he knew everything there was to know
about his bride. She was no longer a mystery. She
became for him a predictable series of responses. She
had become, in his eyes, a known woman.

If he asked for a little in bed, she would take off
her clothes, lie on her back, and only partially open
her legs. Although she meant nothing personal by

this—she had early on explained to him that her libido was weak—he could feel his anger simmer as he parted the ways that allowed him entry to a brief bliss that was never shared by her. The real problem was Nicholas's inability to let the simmering anger he felt at these times exhaust itself. Instead, he let it grow until it became an obstacle and a reason for his growing infatuation with his own impending madness.

He actually believed that whatever he thought of as holding him together was breaking up. He seized upon the fact, yes a fact, that he had to open her legs when he wanted sex as the pivotal reality that unglued the marriage. Unable to express his feelings about this innocent misstep of hers, the fact of the matter grew into an obstacle that he could not overcome. Eventually, his need to express the anger equaled his need for sexual relief. The leg problem was the irritation in the lining of his psyche, and when it eventually took an ugly shape, he was through with sexual relations. He was finished with her.

He then began to pick at the pimples of each day's smallest disconnect. If Beverly took a minute more than her allotted time in the bathroom on work mornings, he would manage to fuss about the slight on his time. If she cut his steak at dinner into slices he considered too thin, he would not only complain but, as time went by, he would make sarcastic remarks about her abilities in the kitchen. In time, the tensions he was causing spread to the children. At first, the verbal pebbles that Nicholas threw into the once calm family waters rippled out on thin waves that left thin marks. In time, though, the arguments of the children with each other grew slightly more self-righteous, and they began to spend less time together. But when they watched their mother cry as the waves grew in volume and speed, it became another story. Aaron stopped watching out for his sister at school and hardly spoke with her at home, which grew thick with silence.

Beverly did the only thing she thought she could to restore the balance of power in the house: she agreed with Nicholas to stop having sex. As bedroom matters had become mechanical by then, this was not a sacrifice for her. For Nicholas, though, it more than took away the every-other-day orgasm to which he had grown accustomed. It took away his rights, his perceived manly rights to her body. The way she agreed inadvertently gave him the excuse he was looking for to leave her. On the night of the refusal, he rolled on top of her, in his mind, for the last time. "Get off me, you fat oaf, and keep that thing away from me. I don't want to see it or have it touch me again."

It was the "again" part of it that most offended Nicholas. He told her in the morning that it was the last straw, that "again" meant forever, and if that was the way she felt about him, he was out of there.

So, he left the next day, without even saying goodbye to the children, without explanation to them. He took a small assortment of files he kept about his work: insurance benefits, pension, that kind of stuff. He left the medium-size box full of photos of their vacations. Beverly noticed that he tossed in the box the photos of her and the kids that he always kept in his wallet. It was his custom to update the wallet photos each year.

His departure was met by the children as a shock and a relief. The social equation at school changed for them. Whereas once they had discussed their parents togetherness with schoolmates of divorced parents with a certain extra sense of security, they were now children of a new station: extra records at school, two sets of addresses and home phone numbers, notes about pickups after school, etc. They would no longer feel an unexpressed superiority over the children who knew separation.

In fact, Aaron and Lisa's situation was not as good as most of their mates whose parents had disengaged, because Nicholas was indifferent to seeing them again. As the divorce proceedings moved along, he never brought up the issue of visitation rights, although he did fight Beverly's request for alimony. He was a smart rat and knew the long-range implications. Not wanting to prolong the argument, Beverly settled for child support in an amount that he could afford, although he knew that for some years to come he would lead the basic life. It was only when he ordered a double bacon cheeseburger after work one day that he realized he had been leading the basic life for his entire marriage. He suddenly realized that he had never given himself the luxury of eating junk food out by himself, just because he felt like it. In fact, he had never allowed himself any self-indulgent luxury.

Because she had been held together at Nicholas's hip by crazy glue, the separation was difficult and painful for Beverly. It was not a clean break. She felt each bit of the parting as if it were a tear or a ripping, every day a new wound, raw and hard to heal. The satisfaction of going to bed and waking up together was gone. His presence on weekends, doodling about the house, the friendly ways he used to have with Aaron and Lisa, shopping together, going to the movies together. All gone now. Without even a wave goodbye.

She didn't realize it when it happened, but the day Nicholas left her was the day she met herself as a woman. She began to make her own decisions, forced at first, yet real. She paid the bills, shopped alone, budgeted, took care of the apartment, and managed the kids. Alone.

In time, the newfound independence fit well. Wondering why she still had feelings for a man as indifferent to her as was Nicholas, she went to a psychologist known for working effectively with women. The work fell into two parts: a probing examination of Beverly's childhood, which was fathomed to be a Petri dish for encouraging dependency, and practical ways to move on.

With this advice, she began to exercise and to get out of the house more often, mostly with a few girlfriends for dinners and movies. She also began to pick up on her relationship with the children by playing board games and video games with them. Her favorite was the hockey game that she and Aaron played often. It was not a game she liked. In fact, she abhorred the violence of the game: the board checking, fighting, bloody noses, teeth knocked out by errant pucks. But it was the only game that made Aaron smile anymore. In all, though, life was getting better.

Until one night right before dinner with the kids, when the phone rang.

"Hi, it's Nicholas." Startled by his voice, Beverly froze.

"Are you there?" he said.

"Yes, I am," she answered.

Whenever she was confused in talking with another, she knee-jerked to politeness, because it seemed reliable and was usually met without an edgy response. Tonight was different.

"Who did you think it was?" he said, before filling in the spaces of her silence. "I guess you thought it was your new boyfriend, the golden boy who took my place. Didn't take you long, did it?"

How do you respond to nonsense? she thought. *By moving on,* she now knew. "Stop being silly. What do you want?" she asked abruptly.

"I want to tell you that I have a brain tumor, and they've given me nine months to a year." As sharp as that, with a tone, she thought, that said, *See, see what you've done,* and, *I told you so.*

"What do you mean, a brain tumor?" was all she could think of saying. At first, she thought this was some kind of perverse joke.

"You know," he answered, sarcasm and venom in his voice. "A big thing, half the size of a peach, inside the left side of my brain. It's rotting away my brain, sucking the life out of me."

He waited for a minute, waiting for her to say

how sorry she was, how much she loved him, how she needed him, how she'd be there by his side to the end. When she said nothing, he resorted to an intellectual expression of his venom, not necessarily toward her alone, although she was a definite part of it. It was directed at life itself, yet mostly at God, who Nicholas believed was responsible for everything, good and bad, in life.

"You see, what it does, the poisonous peach, what it does is it needs blood to keep growing. It wants to grow. So it develops a kind of mouth that sucks whatever is near it, sucks blood from it so it can grow. Like a leech. It sucks the other parts dry, and then they don't work any more. One by one." He couldn't think of anything more horrifying, so he simply said, "Isn't that something?"

"Yes, that's something," she answered so low that he couldn't hear her and asked her to speak up. "What I said was, 'Yes, that is something.' That's all I said."

He continued on to tell her how his writing and speaking abilities would begin to shut down over time, so that near the end he would not want to talk to anyone anymore because the doctors told him he would babble, sort of like a child. "We better talk now because soon there won't be all the time we want," he said, as if there were people out there who had all the time they want.

Beverly knew that if she answered him now that she would start to cry. She didn't want to do that because she figured, she just knew, that he would take advantage. She suddenly felt as if she was caught in a spider's web. She was a good woman, loyal to the man she had once loved and, perhaps, still did. At the same time, she was just beginning to find herself. It was a good feeling. After all the years of dependency, she was finally getting to know herself.

"Where do you live?" she asked, hoping that a question designed to elicit information would take them to a more mundane place.

"I live in a little place near Ditmars," a street she knew was not too far from her. "It's small, but useful. I've got a bedroom, living room, bathroom with a tub but no shower, and a kitchen. Small. Yeah, small." He kept repeating the word as if it defined his life at the moment, but not the peach in his head.

There was something different about him today, a certain begging quality to his voice. It was as if he was beginning to realize that he had been a jerk. Perhaps it was that the tumor had already touched the spot that allows us to know in the deep places of our brains that soon we will be dead.

"Nicholas, I'll call you right back. Give me your number, please." Without hesitation, he gave it to her. She hung up and went to the bedroom, where she sat down on the bed and cried. Deep crying, almost wailing. She then wiped her eyes with a tissue, stroked wayward tears from her left sleeve, and picked up the phone.

"Hello, Nicholas, it's me," she said.

"It's good to hear from you again," he uttered in a pathetic and low tone, as if it had been a long time between conversations.

"Do you mind if I ask you a question?" Without waiting for an answer, she asked him if the tumor was malignant.

"Don't you ever listen?" he blurted out. "Why is it that you never listen to me? I told you, I've got nine months to live. Nine friken months. That's it."

She told him that she was sorry. It was the word he needed to hear.

"Why me?" he shouted into the telephone. "Why me?" he repeated. "I'm forty-one years old, and I'm going to die when I'm forty-two." He began to cry. It sounded to Beverly as if the tears were forced, like a child seeking attention.

"Poor baby." As she said this, she imagined herself stroking his head the way she used to years ago when he was open to her affections. "Poor baby," she said again.

"I'm thinking about going to Sloan-Kettering for an operation. They told me that the tumor is inoperable, but I don't believe them. I believe that if I try hard enough, if I want it badly enough, that I will survive this."

Beverly responded in the way she knew best. "I'll take you, if you want. I'll take you to the doctors, I'll bring you meals, I'll clean your apartment and wash your clothes." When she couldn't think of anything more giving to offer, she said, "I'll even make sure that I open my legs before you have to ask," adding, "but only if you want."

In the quiet desperation of the self-pity that was growing in him, he could only say, "Let's see if I'm up to that." And then he changed the conversation.

"How are the kids? I mean I haven't seen much of them lately."

Trying to hold back the dogs of her tongue from ripping him apart for his neglect, Beverly didn't answer. Even now, though, Nicholas could tolerate silence better than she. Finally, she said, "Aaron could do with your company. He's awfully fond of hockey these days. Maybe you could take him to the Rangers game Thursday night."

Eager to hang onto the only life raft he had left, he said, "Sounds good to me."

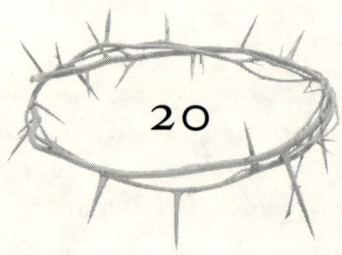

20

THE LETTERS

Francis felt like he was a bit drunk when he arrived home from work and the bar on Wednesday evening, as if one bottle of beer could put him over the edge into a dream world. His perceptions were not too far off the mark.

"It's good to see you, Francis." Of course, it was the voice of Jesus.

Francis was more preoccupied with the amenities he needed to satisfy. Having God sitting on your apartment sofa was not an easy ground to negotiate. "I wasn't sure if you were coming tonight. If I'd have known, I would have something prepared for dinner. As it is..." He stopped, thinking that perhaps he was reprimanding Jesus for not letting him know that he was coming to the apartment.

"It's okay," Jesus said. Just by saying the words,

everything was okay with Francis. "I've been busy and forgot to tell you that I was coming."

"I'm going to order a pizza to be delivered. We can eat while we talk. Do you like pepperoni?"

"Always."

At times like this, Francis would just forge ahead, swimming against the psychic tide of the surrealistic moment.

As soon as they got settled, Jesus said, "If you've got any of that orange juice, can I have a glass?" Francis was quick to oblige.

"Now, let's talk about the letters. I want you to know first that things will have a certain dream-like quality about them for a few days. Time will be suspended now and then. And, as I have told you before, you might not remember everything that will go on. The Father has asked for this. We do not want to start a new reality on earth. That is," he continued in an almost-professorial way, "we would like to energize the people on the earth to know a more vital faith. Yet, we do not want to undermine your most precious gift, your ability to make choices, your free will."

"Why is it that you and the Father … is it all right if I call your father the Father? Or should I say our Father?"

"You could say whatever feels right to you."

They made small talk for a few minutes, the incongruity and refreshing nature of it not lost on Francis. The doorbell rang.

"Please, Francis, be sure to reward the man for his work."

Orange juice and pepperoni pizza with Jesus. Yes, the dreamlike quality was already coming over Francis.

"I want you first to deliver a letter to Richard Darby. We are concerned that he does not have the kind of faith that we'd like. We want him at least to have a fundamental faith. What I mean is faith that our Father is watching out for him, that in spite of everything that goes on or has gone on, that things will work out. This is going to be difficult because there is a 'catch,' as you like to say. There is a chance that his daughter might be killed at the game by an errant hockey puck."

You could have knocked Francis over with a feather. An errant hockey puck!

"I didn't know anything like this might happen—I mean, you asked me to help, and I am deeply honored. But one of my clients might be killed because of these letters. With all due respect, I don't know if I want to be a part of this."

"Francis, I understand how you must feel. But remember it is not the letters that might be harmful. You are only the courier. You are the letter man. A channel for the Father.

"Let me explain. First, you must know that everything will work out okay." He paused to see if Francis was getting this part, that all would be all right in the end.

"Please continue," he said.

"Do you know the Abraham and Isaac story? How Abraham was asked to sacrifice his son?"

"Yes."

"And how everything worked out in the end, after Abraham's faith in the Father was tested?"

"Yes," he repeated, "I know the story."

"It's the same story, only now it's in the twenty-first century. They will each know that something very bad might happen to the flesh and blood they love. A wildly misdirected puck might hit the child in the head and kill him," pausing before saying, "or her."

"But you must tell them that everything will be all right. In return for their trust, each one will have a great faith and will be rewarded abundantly."

He was stunned.

"You can do this, Francis. I know you can. The question is, 'Are you willing?'"

"I think you are asking me to have faith in you that everything will be all right, even if I give them the letters and they go to the game."

'That is what I am asking you."

He knew that Jesus and the Father couldn't lie to him, so he said yes.

"I want Richard to have faith that he is a good man, that my Father does not make garbage. I want him to know that he has been forgiven for his excessive drinking and for his carelessness in the accident. Here's the letter. Read it first."

Dear Richard,

By the time you read this, Francis, your mailman, will have explained things to you. You will know why I am here and what my mission is. I know that most everything about this will be a shock for a while, until you get used to my presence in your life.

Please be certain that everything we ask of you will be met with the support of my Father, your Father. By that, I mean God. You have been chosen because you are trying very hard to overcome your addiction to alcohol. We admire your courage, and we admire your cooperation, that you have accepted the gift of sobriety that has been offered to you.

> With warm regards and much love,
> Jesus

"What do you think?" Jesus asked.

"I don't understand. What does it matter what I think? I am just a man and you are God." Actually, he was thinking that the letter was a bit cold, a little too much to the point.

"How quickly you forget. Do you not remember that the bedrock truth of things, the reality is that the Father, and I ... " He paused, seeming a bit confused to Francis. "Francis, whenever I talk about the Father, I am also talking about me."

"I have already accepted that."

"Good, now what I was about to say is a reminder that you and I, all humans and I, that we co-create the world. Again, it might sound strange to you, but without you and the others, the Father cannot continue to have the world develop according to his vision. He wants the people on earth to evolve toward justice. He wants each person to be drawn to justice. Every time this happens in the life of any one person, the action of that person influences another, and that person another. Goodness spreads. When enough good acts happen, I mean millions, perhaps billions, it is hard to say because the influence of one person is sometimes geometric, then the earth will have met my Father's vision. My Father knows the numbers."

He nodded absently. Somehow, in relating to Jesus, Francis thought it was important to meet his needs for food and drink. "I bought a bottle of wine for you. Would you like a glass?"

"Thank you, perhaps later. I want to get back to co-creating. What I'm saying is that every person counts. That each time a person is kind to another or to an animal, even to a tree, that person is co-creating the world with the Father to where it can be what you call heaven.

"I am not satisfied that Richard is doing much of this. He is aloof from himself and from his daughter. I am going to offer to him a gift of faith. He must first say yes to the offer for it to happen. Tell him that the gift of faith will be offered to him tomorrow at the hockey game, and that his daughter, Erin, will be involved. You must tell him what might happen at the game." And then, as if an aside to Francis, he said, "Of course, I love Richard, yet I am growing weary of him and his selfishness."

Jesus seemed to really enjoy the pizza and was silent for a few minutes while he ate the remaining piece, not even asking Francis if he wanted it. At the same time, Francis was trying to handle his own thoughts about Jesus's fatigue with Richard. It came as a surprise to him that God could be tired of anyone.

"Francis, this is great pie. Let's do it again," he said.

"Now, for the important work. I want you to deliver the letter to Richard today, and I would like you to follow my instructions exactly. First, spend time with him about my visits to you, and my purpose, which is to offer to him the gift of faith. If he doesn't believe what you tell him, do this: wrap your fingers together, then have the pointing fingers connect. You will have to raise them up to do this. Point them toward the sky and say these words, *Oh, God.* When you say the words, a little miracle will occur. Nothing big, but enough to show Richard that you are telling the truth about me.

"Once you have his confidence, tell him that I will offer him the gift at tomorrow night's Ranger's hockey game. He will perk up at this revelation because just this morning Erin asked him, out of the blue, to take her to the game. It will be a surprise because neither one of them follows hockey.

"Again, this is the most important part. Convince him that no matter what happens that everything will be okay." He repeated this several times, each in a slightly different way: *no matter what happens.*

"Go now," he said to Francis. And he went.

Francis didn't know how this was happening, but by now he had such confidence in Jesus that he went ahead. He was delivering the letter to Richard, yet his normal deliveries were not interrupted. Doing God's job and his own became seamless.

It wasn't hard to be welcomed into the apartment.

Richard liked the mailman, perhaps because he was a virtual stranger, a safe person to share his thoughts with. "Thank you for inviting me in." As Francis groped for something to say before telling Richard the purpose of his visit, he noticed the many vases of flowers around the apartment. "I like your flowers," he said.

"Leftovers from my wife's funeral," Richard responded.

"I'm really sorry about your wife's untimely death. I read about it in the newspaper and wanted to tell you how sorry I am." Richard seemed genuinely moved by the overture.

There is no easy way to tell someone that you have a personal message from Jesus for him. So, Francis just sort of blurted it out.

"Mr. Darby," he said, "I have something important to tell you, something that might be difficult for you to accept."

This was not the best way to start, as Richard had heard enough of this kind of "difficult to accept" disclosures recently. "Oh, no," he said, "not another one of those. Please, not another one."

"I am so sorry," Francis responded. "I just don't know of any other way to say this. So, I'll just say it." Richard suddenly seemed to shrink: at first his face, then the rest of him, as if he was a prune losing water.

"God has been in touch with me, and he has asked me to be in touch with you. I don't know why he picked me for this, but he did. He wants you to know that he is not pleased with what he called your selfishness."

This was not the best way for Francis to approach Richard, who was, by temperament and vats of alcohol consumed, prone to be defensive and scared. He was not enthused about what Francis told him.

With a disconcerted look in his eyes, Richard immediately expressed his disbelief. "Sure," he said, "God has decided to get in touch with me through you, a mailman, because he is not pleased with me." With what he thought was a punctuation mark, a dagger of finality to the conversation, he said in the most sarcastic way, "Right!"

"Mr. Darby, I am just a mailman. I deliver mail, that's what I do. Some of my colleagues are polished men and women, but I am not a polished man, so I might not be approaching this the right way. Jesus did not give me any training in how to do this. I see that I'm not doing it right. I should have told you that Jesus is also very pleased with you. He knows that you've had a rotten childhood. He knows how hard you are trying to get well, to stop drinking. He knows that. He knows the courage. That's why he picked you."

"Picked me for what?"

"I hope I can explain this right. He's picked you so he can offer you the gift of faith. I think he means that he wants you to believe in yourself, that you are a good man, that he has forgiven you, and that he wants you to forgive yourself and get on with loving your daughter."

The words seemed to soften Richard. "What does he want me to do?"

"First I'm going to ask you a question. Would you

like to believe that you have been forgiven of anything that you have ever done bad in your life?"

"Well, of course," he answered. "Who wouldn't? I mean who wouldn't?"

"Jesus wants you to know that you have been forgiven by his Father, who is God. I mean, Jesus is God too, but let's not get into that. I don't really understand it. You have been forgiven is the point.

"He also wants you to have faith that everything is going to be okay, even the death of your wife."

"You know, Francis, I have not had a drink in several weeks, but I sure would like one now."

"I hope you don't do that. I really do. Let me get to it. Jesus wants you to know that the gift will be offered to you at the hockey game you will be going to with Erin tomorrow night. Let me tell you that you are going to be faced with a tough choice. If you take her, there is a chance that she will be killed by a hockey puck. One of the players will take a very hard shot, what they call a slap shot, that might hit her in the temple and break a major blood vessel that goes to her brain, and she will die."

Richard stepped back a few steps, as if he had been hit in the head by a hammer. "Does he think I am stupid? In spite of everything, I love her, I really do. She is all I have. I mean, I don't even have myself anymore."

Ignoring the question, Francis said, "That's not all. Please listen to the rest. Jesus wants you to know that whatever happens, it will be for the best, that you will know this in time."

"I don't understand," Richard said emphatically. "I'm getting annoyed." The annoyance began to pull him further from this bizarre conversation. "What if I don't want to play this game? If Erin gets killed, how can everything be all right? I just lost my wife, you know. I'm just beginning to be my old self again, and you tell me that Jesus wants to test me so that I can have faith in myself and in what he promises. Puleeze," he whimpered, "give me a break."

"You've got to remember that there's a good chance that the puck will not hit her. It depends on a lot of things. It'll be like playing a game of pinball. If she walks behind you instead of in front, you know, that'll get her in one seat and not in another.

"I must tell you that you will not be in danger in any of this, so don't worry about yourself. About Erin, though, she would have to sit in Section 9, Row D. I'm not sure what seat the puck might hit her in."

Pulling up the information from his computer was, for Richard, like waiting to see if he had won the lottery of death. "We have seats 13 and 14, Section 9, Row D."

"This still doesn't mean she will be hit. Every detail must be in place: the slight right tilt of her head to avoid the first carom must be the correct angle. Every quickening of the pace must be right. A cold that might slow her down, a bit of extra homework she might do before leaving could change things. Everything must be just right."

"This is crazy," Richard said.

"In the ways that we normally think, maybe it is."

It suddenly occurred to Francis that maybe this *was* crazy. After all, why should Richard even want to have a part in this? He could lose his daughter, and wanting her to live was perhaps the only thing that meant anything to him. The mailman knew that he wasn't equipped to handle this. He just relaxed and asked God to help him, an odd sort of request from someone who did not have much faith himself; that is, until Jesus came into his life.

Richard wanted to throw Francis out, but he did not know how to go about it without offending. Since he stopped drinking a few weeks ago, he had been trying to practice more mature ways to handle his grievances. Most times, when he tried handling things this way, he felt like someone looking for what he needed in a bag that was empty. Mostly, he knew how to get angry.

"Francis," he said, "I am trying to be a good man, and I do not know why Jesus would even be bothered that I do not have faith. I have heard it said that having faith alone is not enough to get us to heaven, that we must do good in the world to be saved. So why should I bother to be concerned about faith? I am trying to do good. I am trying to take care of Erin by being a good man. I think I can be a good man if I don't drink anymore. I cannot drink just a little bit, like other men. Even one drink will have me want another and another. And then, poof, before you know it, I will be a drunk again. I do not want that to happen. *Ever again,*" he said for emphasis.

"Are you trying to tell me that you don't care if you have faith in yourself and in God?"

"I don't really know what I am trying to tell you," he answered, knowing now only that he was confused about all of this.

"Look at it this way, Richard. You want to be a good man. Great. Who would not clap bravo for you? But do you know *why* you want to be a good man?"

"I am not sure. I've never really thought about it. I only know that I am sort of pulled in that direction. Maybe I want to be good because that would be the best for Erin. She won't get hurt. At least by me."

"Do you ever think of heaven and hell?"

"Yes. I think of heaven. And I already know what hell is."

"Do you believe in heaven, Richard? I mean, do you believe that it exists?"

"Yes, I do," he responded. "I am not certain, though. There are days when I believe and days when I don't."

"Then wouldn't you want to have faith in its existence, that God has created a heaven for us?"

"Well, yes, of course."

"Do you have that faith?" Francis asked him. He realized that he didn't know where the words were coming from. Just a minute ago he felt inadequate, and now the questions were tumbling from his tongue.

"Not always," he said, squirming under the onslaught of questions.

"It'd make your life a lot easier if you did," Francis

said back to him before asking him if he knew the story of Abraham and Isaac.

"Yeah, I do. It's the Old Testament. God asked Abraham to take his son up on a mountain where he would be asked to stab him to death, you know, as a sacrifice to God."

Richard was bright, and he was agitated easily. "I think he killed his son, just stabbed him in the heart. And if you think that I am going to kill my daughter by bringing her to a hockey game where she'll get hit in the head by a puck and die because that's the way God wants it, well, count me out."

"I don't know if this makes any difference to you, but you've got it wrong. He didn't kill his son. God stopped him. He was just testing Abraham's faith. When he asked Abraham to kill Isaac, he also told him that everything would be okay. He wanted to see if Abraham believed him that no matter what happened everything would be all right. Just as he was going to stab his son, God told him to stop."

"Look, Francis, you're a nice man. But I wasn't born yesterday. If everything you tell me about what is going on with Jesus visiting you is the truth, I can see the story unfolding here: I'm asked to place Erin in a spot where she can get killed, God asks me to do it anyway, and he tells me that everything is going to be hunky-dory. We'll I'm just not buying. And, besides, your story is preposterous, Jesus coming to Astoria, Queens, to pay us a little visit."

Francis figured it was time to show him the letter. He reached into the bag and slowly drew out the envelope with Richard's name. "Jesus asked me to deliver this to you."

Richard read the letter and responded, "You know, Francis, this is getting worse. How do I know that you didn't type this letter, and that you're just going 'postal' on me?"

It was time for the big one. He pointed his fingers the way Jesus had told him, and said, "Oh, God," loud enough for Jesus to hear, he hoped.

As soon as he said these words, every flower in the vases lifted itself from its stems and began to fly around the room, as if they were invasion boats aligning themselves in the right order to storm Omaha Beach. The rallying point here, though, was about two feet over Richard's head.

This certainly got Richard's attention; more so when they all fell on his head. There he was, sitting with a stunned look on his face, now covered with funeral flowers.

"Do you think it is Shelley trying to talk with me?" he asked.

"I don't know," Francis answered. "Maybe God, maybe Shelley and God. I don't know."

For what seemed like a long time, the two of them fell silent. They just sat and seemed to stare, in some kind of shock. Whatever it all meant, it was certain that a whole bunch of flowers just landed on Richard's head and on the living room floor. No doubt about it, something preposterous had just happened.

"I don't know what to tell you any more," Francis said. "I think you better tell Jesus that you've got to think all of this over very carefully before you decide what to do."

By now, Francis wanted to get out of the apartment. As he got up to leave, he told Richard that he could directly communicate his answer to Jesus. "How do I do that?" a puzzled Mr. Darby inquired.

"It's simple. You just do it. I guess you simply ask him to be with you, to listen to you. And then you tell him what's going on with you."

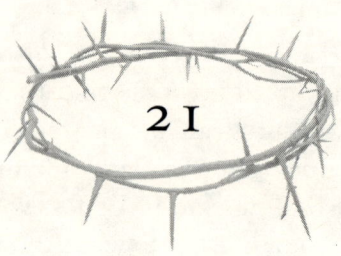

21

Like a giddy kid, Francis said, "That was some trick. You should have seen his face when the flowers fell on his head. He looked like he had just seen a ghost."

Jesus was annoyed. "Francis," he said, "that was not a trick. A trick is intended to deceive. What happened today was a small miracle, a quick suspension of the natural order of things. I told you before, my Father does not want to upset the way things are in nature, though every now and then he will suspend the rules as he did today. Flowers don't fly. You must know that he never forces things in nature or in man. You can always make choices and he will not interfere."

Francis was quick to recover from the feeling that he was back in school. "Let me tell you about today," he said, hoping to avoid another reprimand. "I'm not sure whether Mr. Darby was buying, I mean about you being here and that you're offering to him the gift of faith. But after your little trick, I mean miracle, he said he would think it over and get back to you."

"Okay, good work," Jesus said. "Now, let's get on with Mrs. Aldrich in unit fifty-three. She's a good woman who has gone astray. Not understood at all by her husband, a selfish man who is interested mostly in having things his own way. We are not excluding him from the gifts we offer, but for now we are putting our energy in Cora's, how do you say, basket?"

"I understand what you mean. What do you want me to do?"

"I want you to take the letter I wrote to her, the one with the coal miner stamp on it. It's in the mail that you will deliver today. Ask her to read it immediately, as time, the way you know it, is running out." With these words, Francis felt a surge of fear rise up in his stomach.

"No, Francis, relax. I am not talking about the end of the world. What I mean is that the game is tomorrow night, and we must do some fast work here. I don't want to totally suspend time."

"But Mrs. Aldrich—s-she's a temptress."

"A temptress, you say. Well, aren't you getting biblical," Jesus responded before staring at Francis with an amused look on his face.

"Well, what I mean to say—"

"I know what you mean to say: that she's been a bit of a slut. When I was beginning my Father's mission, there was talk going around about a woman named Mary Magdalene and me, that she was a whore and my girlfriend. It was a kind of what you call today 'a smear campaign.'"

"So, I should just discount that she is coming on to me?"

"I'm not saying that, Francis, and I'm not saying I approve of what she does. What I am saying, what I am asking you, is to not be so fast in judging her. She has reasons for making overtures to you. Perhaps they are as innocent as that she needs someone to talk to, something which she does not get anymore from her husband. It might not mean that she wants to lie in your bed. You tend to put most everything in little boxes. It makes life less complicated for you to put Mrs. Aldrich in a box you call *slut*. Then, whenever you get a little confused about her or what she does, you place her there. Putting her there means she's a bad person, she's a sex addict, she's irresponsible, a bad mother. Fill in the rest. You're good at that. You could use some faith yourself." He finished with a flurry, and not a small amount of sarcasm, or so Francis thought.

"Here, read the letter I have sent to her," Jesus abruptly directed.

Dear Mrs. Aldrich,

By now you will know that I am Jesus, and that I am here in Astoria. I have asked Francis, your mailman, to intercede for me. He is a special friend of mine who is helping me to do the work of our Father who is in heaven.

We know that you are having a difficult time, and that you have lost faith in yourself, as well as in all the beautiful things you once believed in, especially when you fell in love with Bob and got married. Back then, you believed in the future. You trusted Bob and yourself. He might want to call you vain for having your nose fixed. In reality, he was as angry as a little boy because he was upset that you did not listen to him and do what he wanted.

I know that for a while now you have not been keeping the standards you once set for yourself. You have betrayed your marriage vows. You do not seem to understand that each time you transgress you diminish yourself, your trust, your faith.

You have been picked for a special mission because you are a very good and sincere woman who is now lost, but is trying to embrace her values once again. When I was on the earth many years ago, I spoke with my followers about the wayward son. You are not unlike him.

When you are done reading this letter, Francis will tell you about the gift I am offering to you. If you are willing to accept this gift, your life will change. It will get better. You will find yourself again.

With respect and affection,
Jesus

"You are not to reveal ever or to anyone what you have learned from this or any letter, Francis. Do you understand me?"

He understood precisely what Jesus meant. He was to tell no one that Cora had become a weak woman.

When Jesus told Francis that he was sometimes going to suspend time, play with it a little bit, he

GERARD BROOKER

wasn't making hyperbole. Suddenly, Francis was in
unit fifty-three, talking with Cora Aldrich. After he
introduced his presence as best he could, he handed
the letter to Cora.

"Here is the letter from Jesus. Before I go any further, he wants you to first read it."

She took the letter. Francis was impressed with
how fast she read. "Okay, I read it. Now what?" she
asked abruptly. He was surprised at her indifference.

"I know that you will be taking Angelina to a
hockey game tomorrow night," Francis said. He was
surprised when he began to feel a bit apprehensive
that Cora was getting very serious. He'd expected that
she would try to flirt with him now. Those were the
grounds of expectation, and when she didn't, he felt
off his mark.

"Mrs. Aldrich, I'll cut right to the chase." She had
heard the last part of that a few times in the past few
months. "Jesus is asking you to risk Angelina's life at
the hockey game in return for the gift of faith. In fact,
if you say yes to him, you will be acting in faith. I
mean you will be trusting God. Before you answer, he
wants you to know that everything will be okay with
Angelina if you accept the offer."

"You know, Francis, I don't know what in the
world you're talking about. Would you like a beer,
maybe slow down?" she blurted out, as if he needed
some help with his thinking processes.

"No, not really. I'm working now. No drinking
allowed during work hours."

He proceeded to explain to Cora how Angelina

might be hit by a puck that could break a blood vessel in her head and kill her. And, for that to happen, how everything needed to be aligned, whether she sat in one seat or another, went for a hot dog or not, stayed the extra seconds to put mustard on it or not, and so on. That the gift of faith Jesus wanted to offer Cora could be hers if she said that she would take Angelina to the game and take Jesus's word for it that everything, no matter what happened, would be okay.

Cora was a quick study and got it right away.

"You know, Francis, I used to be a pretty good person, a little vain maybe, but no big deal. Then when things went wrong between Bob—that's my husband—and me, well, I couldn't see the light at the end of the tunnel anymore. I just began to sink into nothingness. I wanted so much to have Bob in my life. I wanted to be loved, have someone to care about me, hug me. When he withdrew from me, I started to look elsewhere. And I wasn't much of a mother anymore."

Francis knew some of this, as much from the letter as from her flirtatious ways that went over the line. He thought he would tell her that he knew, that this might add to her confidence in him as the messenger of Jesus. He figured, though, from the admonition that Jesus had given to him about confidences, that he'd better play this one on the safe side.

"All I have in my life now is Angelina. How could I leave my Angelina open to being killed and believe that everything will be good? How could I be certain of that? There is no evidence for what I am being asked."

"I wish I knew what to tell you. Just because Jesus has asked me to deliver these letters and to help a bit doesn't mean that there's anything special about me. I'm just a mailman; in fact, a guy who also needs a shot of faith.

"What I do know is that from the few times I have had together with him—you know, to talk—he's the real deal. What I mean is he means what he says, and you can count on him to back it up. He's even given me a way that I can ask him to provide a little miracle."

"I don't want a little miracle," she responded. "All I want is my Angelina."

"That's a good thing," Francis said, agreeing with her. "Sometimes, I think that providing someone with a little miracle as a way of proving his point is a little unfair to others who don't get to have a miracle." He didn't know why he said this. Maybe it was because of a negative vibe that he was picking up lately from Jesus.

"On the other hand," he said, "a gift's a gift."

There was no easy way to do this, Francis knew. He tried telling her about conversations he had had with Jesus about faith, that it usually came about after a person had been beaten down a lot. It didn't have to be that way, but that was the usual way.

"Most of us, you know," he said, "try hard to figure everything out. But many things do not make sense. Why does this family get killed passing through an intersection and not that one who passed through the same place the night before? Why does this man get stabbed to death by a drugged robber and not the first guy who passed by him in the shadows? Is it fate?"

She stopped him. "Francis, what in the heck is fate? I know you say it's destiny, it's what's supposed to happen. I mean, who says what is supposed to happen. Is it God? Some spirit in the universe? I don't think it's God. I mean, what an awful God it would be to have Mr. Smith, the father of five kids, stabbed to death by a crazed man. That's no God. That's a force with whimsy."

She stopped to breathe. It was obvious that she had, at one time or another, given this a great deal of thought.

"I don't want to think of God as a needy something, you know? Someone that gets satisfaction out of hurting a person. That's no God, either.

"And then," she said, "if I think that all these random evil things happening to one guy and not to another, then I think it's a stupid, messed-up world we live in. Maybe it's a place that we should just disown in our brains, a place that makes no sense at all. Just get on with it, you know. Live in it, but not make anything out of it."

"I hear you, Mrs. Aldrich," he said. "I think, though, you gotta think of how that all stacks up inside yourself. I mean, do you really want to just blow off the world while you're living in it? I mean, I guess there are lots of people who do that. But, I don't know if they are happy inside themselves doing that. People are all around us, and maybe blowing them off inside ourselves can make us crazy. I don't know if you want to kiss off all the people at your job, you know, the doctors and nurses. I've got to think that some of them are good people, people you'd trust in a pinch."

By now, Cora was very confused. She didn't even know why she allowed herself to enter this conversation. So heavy. So, like a knee smacked with a hammer, she jerked to the place where she had been somewhat comfortable. She began to seek the darklight. "I've got a nice new rendition of a great Spanish song called 'Guantanamera.' I'm going to play it so you and I can dance. It's still a little light out, so I'm going to shut off this lamp."

Like most men finding themselves in these circumstances, Francis felt a twinge in his loins. Although he didn't want to acknowledge what he felt, his body spoke the words for him: *Here's a chance to get some, right now, today.*

Yet, he tried to keep a sense of himself, that he was a special person in Jesus's mission, even though he didn't want to see himself as a "special person." He was torn between the longings of a man who had been without a woman for a long spell and his desire to complete today's assignment.

As soon as she put the CD on her player, she pressed the "repeat" button. It seemed like a long time ago when she and Bob made love with feeling. Ironically, the song about a woman spurned always made her feel romantic. Again, she offered Francis a glass of wine. Again, he refused, as a kind of gesture to keep his resolve. But he was fast sinking into the growing surge of his needs, and he knew it.

She took her own glass in hand and said to him, "Let's dance," more an order than a request. He told himself that having one dance with her might mollify her edginess. One dance to the tune led to another, and soon he felt himself under the spell of the moment. He soon forgot about everything except to tend to the urgencies he felt within.

When they finished, Cora told him how satisfied she felt, that she had a "connection" to him, unlike the way she felt toward other men she had known recently. Several minutes after he regained his breath, Francis got up quickly, dressed, and left, not remembering why he had come to Cora's apartment in the first place.

Halfway down the stairs, he remembered before being overcome by another temptation: would he tell the truth to Jesus?

Before Francis had a chance to say anything, Jesus told him that he'd next have to deliver two letters at once.

"I want to hurry this up. I don't want to suspend time too much, because doing that might give the impression that everything we are doing here is under the direction of exclusive divine power. That is not the impression our Father wants to give, nor is it what is happening. He is offering the gift of faith through me, and you are the channel. But everyone we are extending our hand to must accept the gift, must say yes, or else nothing will happen. Remember, however, that each person is free and can say yes or no. We are co-creators of the evolution of the world." He was preaching.

"Before we go any further, I have something to tell you. I don't have an answer from Mrs. Aldrich. I did something, well, something maybe bad."

"I know," Jesus said abruptly. "You failed yourself and your mission on our Father's behalf. You failed Mrs. Aldrich by giving in to her. She's got to stop turning to sex to straighten out her life. She's got to believe in herself. She's got to have faith. Your job was to explain to her what I am doing here, tell her about the gift she is being offered, and to try to get an answer from her. So what do you do, instead?" There was no need for Francis to answer.

"Francis," he said, "you must know where Astoria Park is. I want you to meet Bill Waxman and Tina Remsen there at two o'clock this afternoon. Here are the letters for you to deliver to them first."

Could it be that he was being just like any other person? It seemed so.

"Read them if you want. Or not," Jesus said to him. "I don't care."

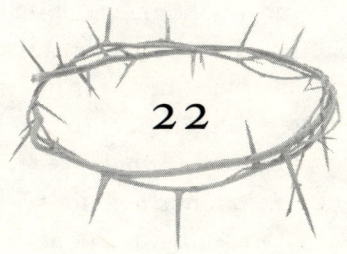

22

The walk to the park took Francis about a half-hour. He had taken the same route hundreds of times as a kid, especially on Saturday mornings when the big pool was opened for free. Today, though, he was sad that he had failed Jesus, who seemed angry with him.

Any diversion on this day was a good diversion. He began to think about how the neighborhood had changed since he was a kid. He remembered the old men, who always seemed tough to him, playing board games under the Triborough Bridge. How he liked it when one of them would spring up like a jungle cat to pounce on one of the young toughs who liked to taunt them, just because they could. The games tables were empty today. *It would be good*, Francis thought, *if the old guys were still around to box a few ears.* He guessed there were still the old men—there would always be old men—but they didn't hang out much with each other any more. Probably home watching TV shows.

He remembered how the ice cream trucks came around, ringing their sweet bells for moms to fork up a nickel for plain, ten cents for deluxe, and the delight he used to get out of hitting the bare legs of women across the street on summer evenings with his B-B gun. Or dropping water-filled balloons from rooftops on the heads of shoppers walking their wares home on a Friday night. And the ice-cream shops where the cool guys hung out with their girls, who liked to taunt him when he passed. He thought about the people sitting on their stoops, watching the world go by. Even as a kid, he loved the inaction of those people, constant and stable. You could count on them being there.

When he got to the edges of the park, he stopped to reflect once again before walking up the slight incline that led to the ball fields. He remembered the many games he played here as a kid. And the day his dad came to see him play, the only time. He remembered that he got the base hit that broke up a no-hitter late in the game, the day he made a spectacular over-the-head catch in center field. To this day, he couldn't believe that he had made a catch equal to the great Willy Mays.

A little hi and a dark hello greeted him, and the reverie was over. It was Tina and Bill. She was cheerful enough, but Bill was in a bad mood. "Young man," he said to Francis, "I hope I'm not on a wild goose chase, some kind of U.S. Postal Service joke. There better not be cameras set up to watch me make a fool of myself. Wouldn't sit good with me."

Tina interrupted. "I'm Tina Remsen. We don't know each other, but I know you, a sort of public figure on the block, you realize. Mr. Waxman and I have both received a letter in the mail. We met coming here. He seemed to be upset when he told me that he was coming because he had received a letter from Jesus, a funny sort of letter."

Francis invited them to walk with him toward an area where there were picnic benches and places to sit in the grass under a canopy of pine trees that lined the rim of the park. Without a word, they sat at one of the tables, as if it had been prearranged.

"I want to tell you," Francis said, "that I have not read either one of the letters. When I last left Jesus, he was in a sort of a mood. He was angry with me, I think, because of something I had done. I think that was yesterday, but I'm not sure. I've been losing track."

He might have been Jesus himself talking to them, such was their bewilderment at what he was saying.

"I've got so many things to say to you. This might not be the best way for me to start, but Jesus sometimes does strange things with time. I mean it goes forward fast, or backwards, and at times it just doesn't go anywhere."

"What in Jesus's name do you mean it just doesn't go anywhere?" Waxman asked.

"I don't know," an annoyed Francis responded. "It stays still, I guess."

He decided to deliver his orders as briefly as he

could. *The story I have to tell is so far out,* he thought, *that a person would either believe it or not, no matter what I say.*

"Let me tell you that a while back, Jesus came to my apartment right here in Astoria, where I live, not too far from both of you. Don't ask me why he came to me. I cannot give you an answer. He told me that his Father—who is in heaven, I might add—is disappointed that so many people on earth, especially here in America, do not have much faith anymore. I think he means faith in the goodness of the Father, and I think he means faith in themselves, that having things is not the answer.

"He thinks that the two of you are special people, and that you both are undergoing a sort of spiritual crisis." He paused before looking straight at Bill who was sitting directly across from him.

"Bill, I know that you think the men you killed never answer your prayers for forgiveness. If you had faith in God, you would know that he has forgiven you, even before the words are formed in your head. If you had faith in the afterlife, you would know that the men you killed on Iwo Jima have forgiven you. I know now from talking with Jesus that the place we like to call heaven is so different from what we know here that our language is mostly inadequate to explain it. I get the idea, though, that it's a state of great awareness, a way of being that is full of grace. What I mean is that it's where, well, not *where.* I mean it's not a place like we know places. Anyway, I hope this makes sense to you."

It was clear that Bill was annoyed at these ideas, which were way out for him. "I've got to take a little walk," he said.

"Good," Francis answered. "It'll give me a chance to talk with Tina."

As Bill got up, bothered by the arthritis in his left hip, they watched him limp his way toward his own inner world that up to now, with the exception of periodic intrusions that he allowed Jane and Megan, was as heavily protected as a concrete pillbox on Iwo Jima.

"He's a really nice man," Tina said, adding, "but he seems sad."

Francis did not know what to say to this. He asked her about the letter from Jesus.

"Well, it got my attention. I thought it was a joke, especially the part about looking at the stamp dedicated to miners. I figured it might be National Joke Week at the post office. You know, tell a joke on one of your clients, jazz things up a bit at the office stuff. The letter makes him sound, well, so human.

"Most people would like to think he was only God, but they don't realize that he was also a man, a real man, like I'm a man. That at the same time he is God, he knows and feels and thinks like a man. People seem to understand and appreciate his crucifixion, how tough and painful it was. Yet, they won't accept the other parts of his humanity. They only want to know the pain, the miracles, the nobility of it all. But they can't stand to bear the weight of his fullness as a man."

"Wow," she uttered.

"Mrs. Remsen, I know that your son is included in Jesus's plan to offer you the gift of faith."

"Yes, he also explained in the letter that if I take Christopher to the hockey game on Thursday night, that something awful might happen to him, that he might be killed by a puck coming into the stands. But that everything will be okay, as long as I have faith that it will be okay. But I don't know. I mean, how can I put my son in jeopardy so that I might have faith?"

Then she said the most astonishing thing. "Why would I want to have faith at that price? I mean, faith in what? I don't even know what he is talking about. It's such a vague thing, this faith. I don't know what he means. Quite frankly, Francis, I try to be a good person, even though I have been abandoned by my husband who's here, you know, but he's not here.

"If Jesus is talking about faith in him, in the Father, I think that I might have that already."

"I think he's talking about something way beyond that, Mrs. Remsen." She stopped him to ask if he would call her Tina from now on. "What I'm trying to say, Tina, is that Jesus is talking here about a kind of extraordinary faith." Then he asked her if she read the Bible.

"Yes, I do, sometimes."

"Do you now the story of Abraham and Isaac?"

"I do. Something about God asking a big shot named Abraham to sacrifice his son by stabbing him to death. And then he didn't have to stab him. God stopped him as a reward for believing in him."

"You've got most of the essentials right. What you didn't get, perhaps," adding the word *perhaps* so as not to sound insulting, "is that Abraham and God had a very good, a very excellent relationship before he was asked to sacrifice his son. I think that maybe without your knowing it, that you have a very good, maybe excellent, relationship with God also, and that he is asking you to have an extraordinary faith here."

Tina never thought of herself as having a great relationship with God. Sure, she prayed to him. Fact is, she knew that she talked with him lots during the day, had a regular ongoing talk, yet it was one way, not really a dialogue.

"If I have this great relationship, why don't I ever hear from him? Look now, I don't mean to say I expect to hear his voice or anything like that. It's just that after trying for so long, I think I'm just talking into a void. Now, I just don't get this about God. I mean, why the mystery? Why doesn't he talk to us? At least every now and then, I mean."

The last part was not a question. It was a statement of how she thought things ought to be. Just as she was about to say more, an angry Bill Waxman came back.

"Look here, young man, I've been thinking about what's going on. I get a letter from Jesus, I guess, and in it he asks me to take my Megan to the hockey game, where she might get killed. I mean, does he think I'm some kind of jerk, or something?

"Take Megan to get killed!" He puffed a huff. "Doesn't this god of yours who writes letters know that I have seen killing, that I have killed men. So he wants me to take little Megan to get hit in the head with a puck hard as a bullet. I've seen men with their heads blown off and he wants me to take her into a battle zone!"

"Please sit down."

"I precisely do not want to sit down," he answered. "Do you know how many times I have asked God to forgive me for killing those Japs on Iwo Jima? Well, I'll tell you, lots, that's how many times, lots of times. I ask and I ask, and I never hear a thing back."

Francis could imagine him on Iwo, running around, killing half-dead men in caves. It didn't take a leap of the imagination. *He's a tough guy,* Francis thought, *probably just as tough on himself as on anyone else.*

"Maybe all you have to do is forgive yourself," Francis said to him, "and then God'll forgive you."

"Tried that," he said. "Tried it and it didn't work. I thought it did, at least for a while, but then when Jane died, it kept coming back. Just kept coming back."

"You've got to have faith, Mr. Waxman, that God is a good god. That he has forgiven you."

"How can I believe that, young man? If he's such a good god, why didn't he keep on eye out for Ned on Iwo? You know, there's never been a man as good as Ned, and he gets shot, right in the mouth. Just dead, bam, like that," he burst out, trying to snap a sound of finality from his old fingers.

There was no answer. Not from Francis, not from Tina, not from God. There was only a soft sobbing sound that came from somewhere in Bill's lower throat as if it was, too, a cave that echoed the groans of long ago and somehow needed to be quieted.

"I'm going home," Bill said. "You tell that god of yours that I just don't get it. I try hard. But I just don't get it. And while I'm at it, young man, I hope you know how lucky you are. God speaks to you. That's more'n the rest of us get."

"I'll walk you home, Mr. Waxman. It's a long way," Tina said. She turned to Francis. "I'm just as confused now, maybe more confused, than I was half an hour ago. I just don't know if I want to jeopardize Christopher. I really don't know what I'd get for taking the chance."

She took Bill by the arm, looked back at Francis, and said, "See ya."

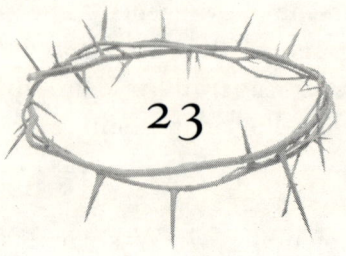

23

NICHOLAS

By now, the peach sucking the life out of Nicholas's brain was only a few days bigger than when we first met him. In the big scheme of things, a few days didn't seem like much. Yet, a few more grains of sand had gone from the top portion of his hourglass to the bottom. In that Nicholas was given fewer grains to begin with, a few days were countable, bringing him predictably closer to his death.

Let's play a little "God" here ourselves by pushing the story several months into the future after Nicholas went to Sloan-Kettering for an operation. When it was over, the surgeon, in solemn tones, told Beverly that they had removed much of the massive tumor. He called it "de-bulking" the tumor. It was a doctor's set speech, the one designed to let loved ones know that all that could be done had been done, yet please be prepared for the slow, relentless onset of death. As the peach would grow again, it would need to eat again. It was clear, as the weeks wore on and Nicholas's in-town doctor continued to prescribe a reduced plan of chemotherapy, that only a miracle could cure him.

Normally, Nicholas didn't think much about miracles. He'd never experienced one, but he'd read about them. When a friend told him that he had access to a piece of bone of a holy man, now dead, who had founded a religious order, and that the congregation was looking for a miracle born from prayers to the holy dead man, he was happy to wear the relic around his neck for some time until, without results, he was asked to give it back.

He told Beverley that he really didn't expect much from the attempt at a miracle, as these were meant for those who had faith that their prayers would be answered. Nicholas knew that he had little or no faith in anything anymore, especially that God would answer him.

If prayer is talking with God, then Nicholas was praying. He was slowly coming to accept that he was going to die soon, yet it became increasingly important to him to know why, at such a young age, a hungry peach was growing in his head. He kept asking, "Why me?" and he kept receiving silence as his answer.

This, in turn, kept him churning inside, removed from the peace he hoped might be his before he died. He was becoming churlish and irritable. Whereas once he was courteous, even flirtatious, with his nurses, he now became demanding. The coffee was never hot enough, the food without seasoning. Even though he tried to be more present to Beverley, Aaron, and Lisa, he began to grow more aloof the closer he came to his end. These are things you ought to know about Nicholas. By knowing, his response to Jesus's letter is clearer than it might have been. Here is the letter Francis gave to him.

Dear Nicholas,

I am asking you at the beginning here to please continue to read this letter. I know that you are angry with me, but I want you to know that you are closer to me than most people. I am sad that you do not realize it.

I know that you are angry with me because I have not answered your question about why it is you who has terminal cancer. I have not answered your question because I do not have an answer that would make sense to you.

You want to make the Father responsible for everything that happens on earth. I mean everything, the good and the bad alike. I'll try to explain a little bit how it works with our Father. Let's start with you. The tumor that you have in your head was not put there or started by him. There is this great force of nature that sometimes does weird things in the world. One of those things is disease, including, of course, cancer. The way of the world has been to upset the natural well-being of human bodies. So many chemicals, so much pollution and radiation. You are a victim of that.

The Father has chosen—I'll use the word "chosen" because it's the closest word to what really happened—to let every consequence of your chosen actions run its natural course.

Now, here's the difficult part. The intellect of even the smartest humans is most limited. I know you like to do this IQ thing. But, I've got to tell you that even if one of you had an IQ of 900, you still would be considered a moron in relation to the Father. I do not say that to belittle humans. We know that God does not make junk.

The way your brains are set up does not allow you to accept contradictions. You, Nicholas, know only that malignant brain tumors are bad, that with yours, your time on earth is limited. What you do not know, the ecstasy you cannot know without faith, is that a tumor like this is not evil. People of the earth like to think that evil is wherever good doesn't show up. And since there is no goodness in a bad tumor, well, I think you've got the point.

Surely, the Father does not make it happen that you are dying at a young age. So, do not ask him "Why me?" any more, as it is a wasted question to which, in your inability to hold contradictions as true, there is no answer. Except if you have faith that the Father always loves you. In fact, he is in love with you. I say that not in the usual sense, of course, but so that you can understand the power of his love for you.

If you remember the first days of being in love with Beverley, how the sun revealed the beauty of her soul, you would know a little of what the Father sees in each of you here on earth. Do you know he actually does know the number of feathers on each bird's head? Ah, then, how much more does he love you, Nicholas Street?

I will be direct with you. Your son, Aaron, might be accidentally killed by a puck at the game tomorrow night. If you take him, you run that risk. But if you believe that everything will be all right if he is killed or not, then you will stand beside the great Abraham as a man of faith.

Please let Francis know if you will bring Aaron to the game.

With a love beyond understanding,
I Am Jesus

"Nicholas, you seem bewildered. He can do that," Francis said.

"I don't know what to say."

Actually, he did know what to say, yet didn't know if he should say it. *The letter from Jesus is magnificent, that is, if written for a holy person,* he thought. But, Nicholas never had considered himself to be holy person. Because he had been denied a miracle, he thought of himself as an unholy person, one not worthy. He was convinced that God granted miracles only to very worthy people.

For a long time Nicholas thought that God had favorites. Without knowing it, he had cultivated a sense that having favorites was undignified. Until recently, he had been afraid to express the anger he felt except in the privacy of prayer, and only in the past few days. Now he could have the chance to speak, perhaps directly to God, about the growing insults he was feeling. He knew with clarity that he was not one of God's chosen individuals. He was a leftover, one of the billions of the masses who were not worthy of private attention.

Because of the possibility to meet Jesus and say these things, he began to get a little manipulative. He decided to pretend he was interested in offering up Aaron as a possible sacrifice. Maybe, then he'd have the chance to meet Jesus face-to-face.

Normally, God would allow a man like Nicholas, who was slowly losing control over his mental functions, to think that he was duping him. Yet another contradiction was playing out. Before Nicholas could even formulate the words he would freely say, God knew what the words were.

Disregarding the usual ways of the Father, Jesus decided to appear to Nicholas. "Hello, Nicholas," Jesus said, offering his hand. It would be apparent to most people that this was Jesus, at least a good facsimile of him. But Jesus knew the circumstances for this man in front of him were not the best. He was suffering, and if there was a "doubters" club, he would have had a first-class membership.

"How do I know you're Jesus?" he asked.

"You don't. You could ask Francis here, but all I can do for you is to say I am the one who wrote the letter. I offer to you a little miracle. Only a little one, mind you. In fact, so tiny that you could probably make a case that it's a trick, a bit of magic. Nevertheless, it's the best I'll do for you right now. I want to make your special acquaintance. I mean in the way we normally don't until after a person dies and is reborn into a new state of being."

Francis, always intrigued by the possibility of a miracle, waited.

"Before the miracle, I must first ask you, Nicholas, what is the color of the room we are sitting in?"

"It's a light yellow," he answered.

"And what of those flowers in the vase by the TV set?"

"They're not real flowers. Just fake red roses. I like fake ones. They last longer."

Jesus got up from his chair and walked across the living room, the place where Nicholas spent most of his last days, thinking and smoking cigarettes. "Blink your eyes," he directed Nicholas, who did as he was told. "Now, look at the color of the room we are in."

"My God," Nicholas gasped.

"Yes, indeed," Jesus said with a knowing smile. "And smell your roses. Put your hands on them." He did as he was told.

"It appears as if you are Jesus, or at least someone like him," Nicholas murmured, as if the admission had been tortured out of him.

"Let's go for a walk. It's stuffy in here." The maggoty smell of the dying who had ceased tending to the hygienic needs of their bodies was in the air.

Nicholas could hardly walk, his body so bloated with the effects of the chemo treatment he had received. "Can I help you?" Jesus asked. It had taken Nicholas many months and several falls before he acquired the humility to say yes to an offer like this.

"Please just hold onto my arm," he replied, limping toward the elevator, which would take them nine floors down to the street. And then Jesus decided, who knows why, to do another little miracle. Perhaps it was because he loved Nicholas so. When the door to the elevator opened, Jesus held onto Nicholas's arm so tightly that he couldn't move toward the door.

"Watch the doors close," he commanded. "Now, watch them open." Quickly, they opened, and he directed Nicholas again. "Turn around. We're here."

Jesus, who was starting to know the neighborhood, suggested that they walk along Grand Avenue, one of the main streets in Astoria. The avenue was busy, but the negative energy of anxiety was in the air.

"There is much tension in the streets today," Jesus remarked. "I can feel it in my own head. Perhaps because I am with you."

Nicholas would retain the language of the street until the very end.

"Whad'ya mean by that?" he asked.

"I mean that I think I am losing you."

"Well, I think you are," Nicholas answered. "Jesus, I know I ought to be afraid of you. I am more convinced than I am not convinced today that you are Jesus, the Son of God. But, I also believe that I can speak the truth to you."

People along the street were staring at them. Car horns honked angrily as traffic slowed down to let drivers and their passengers steal a look at what might have seemed to them an incongruous sight: an obviously sick person shuffling along with the aid of a biblical-looking man who could pass for the stereotypical Jesus of the ancient world of artists' renditions.

"I know that you have power over life and death, and Francis has explained to me about Aaron and the hockey game. But I *am* angry with you. You know it's mostly because of my cancer and that you never answer my prayers. I'm angry because other people get cured, and I don't. I'm mad because you seem to have favorites. And, to be sure, I am not one of them.

"So, I decline your offer to put Aaron at risk. I most decidedly decline to be tested on behalf of my son. I like to think I love him as much as I can, and that is very little. I am not capable, as you probably know, of loving much. I was born selfish, and I haven't grown much in that regard. In fact, I sometimes I think that I'm going crazy. I just don't believe in anything anymore. I'm going to take a pass on your offer. And I hope that you won't punish my son because of my decision. He is a good boy and worthy of your love, far more worthy than I am or ever was."

Because Jesus had chosen to be totally human on this visit, he found it hard to respond. "I want to tell you that I am sad, Nicholas. Each day, our Father offers the gift of faith, sometimes just a small favor, a push ... I think you call it grace here ... toward faith in him, and a lot of the times the offer is refused. Of course, I am sad when that happens. Though I am with the Father, I still retain my humanity, so I can still be sad. So many people ask me in their prayers where I was when the Holocaust of the Jews occurred. Many of them specifically ask me about the children, the thousands and thousands of children who died at the hands of the Nazis. The innocent children who had not yet lived their lives.

"Where was I? Where was the Father? I will speak for myself. I was for a long time doing a sort of crying, though it was beyond crying. I can only give you an example of what I mean how it was beyond, a little like the brilliant sensitivity in the life after this one that you will know.

"I will tell you a story," Jesus said. "A man who died not so long ago came to the Father with an ecstasy that was beyond the usual. His concern was that his beloved wife, who had died of a cancer not unlike yours, was also in this holy place. We knew that he loved her in a way that almost seemed beyond human capacity. So, the Father was especially happy to meet him and to talk closely with him.

"'Your wife is here,' the Father told the man, 'and she will be with you shortly.' The man began to look transformed, beyond what usually happens at the arrival in the place of their greatest expectations. His happiness at knowing his wife was there was, let's say it so you can understand, palpable.

"The Father said to the man, 'Your love for your dear wife, Sheila, is evident. She makes you whole. The path toward real love on earth is rarely completed. It is not that we have made it deliberately difficult. It just seems to be that way for almost everyone. Yet, it is not beyond reach, and you have done this. We know your story, but please tell it again because I love to hear it.

"'It is not a stunning story for me to tell. In the

first year of our dating, Sheila and I went to a concert one summer evening just outside of Rome.

"'It was all there, I mean, everything a man could ask for was there that night. The weather was beautiful, warm and breezy, the moon hung over the ancient ruins where the band sat tuning their instruments. I think it was the light. You know, the evening light that Italians love to talk about, the light that sets things apart in a pink kind of clarity. For a second, it was shining directly onto Sheila's face when my eye caught the wisp of a hair hanging from her head. Anyhow, the way it fell against her cheek made her look like a work of art. And then she caught me staring at her. When I looked at her, the last rays of that same light made her eyes appear to be expressions of grace and charm. She was more beautiful than any woman I had ever seen.

"'I don't have to say how struck I was by this. I was in love with her, that I knew. But when the orchestra began to play, something special happened, something never again repeated. It didn't have to be repeated. What I felt was so strong that it never left my heart.

"'I put my hand around her shoulder and placed it against her arm. The music started and the singing began. Frankly, I didn't know a word of what they were saying. But, the music was soft and gentle. I didn't know what I was doing, but I began to press the palm of my hand against her upper arm, sort of massaging it. It began to get... I hope you don't mind my saying... sexual for me. So I stopped. But I couldn't stop. The strangest thing, the most wonderful thing, hap-

194

pened. I began to know the essence of this extraordinary woman.'

"'What I am trying to say is that I knew at that moment the entirety of who she was. I knew her beauty, of course. That was always easy, but it is not what I am talking about. I mean, I knew her spirit, I knew her being. It is the only way I can say it. Yes, I knew her being.

"'The closest I can come to telling you what I knew is that it was like an aroma, an extraordinary aroma, the kind that makes a person feel good. Maybe a little like the smell of a freshly diapered baby with talcum powder. Not really, though. More like a special sweetness I had never known. I want to say that I knew the wonder of her. But it was beyond what the poets say. It was more than any truth or goodness I had known. I knew her. It is hard to explain. I felt as if for a moment that I had been given a special gift beyond my senses, perhaps a sense unknown to us. I can't tell you more, as I do not have the words.

"'What I can tell you is that from that moment on, I was always in love with her. In a way, you might say, I never exhausted my infatuation with her. For over sixty years, mind you.'"

Nicholas was deeply impressed with the story, more with the man who loved his wife beyond understanding than with Jesus's attempt to explain to him how sad he was about the children who died in the Holocaust.

"I hope I have answered your question about where I was during the Holocaust. I was crying, filled with the love I am trying to explain in a way that you can grasp."

Nicholas began to shake his head back and forth, as if the answer, new and different, was bothering him. "But where were you?" he asked, stuck in the question. Again, Jesus answered that he was crying because we had once more violated his basic command to love one another.

"Strange answer," Nicholas said. And then he said, "Whatever."

Jesus had only to hear the resignation in his voice to know what that word meant.

When Nicholas wanted to talk again about how angry he was that the peach in his head was about to kill him at such a young age, Jesus reminded him that he had lived for some time, and that the gift of life was unearned.

"You might be grateful for your life, instead of complaining," he said. "It might sound funny to you for me to say this, but I'm speaking for myself as a man when I say how tired I have become at the complaints that come to me every day." He paused, before saying, "Yours too."

"I can understand that you might be upset with me. I probably seem ungrateful to you. But all I want is my equal share. The average guy in America lives about seventy-seven years. That's thirty-plus more than I am now. So, the way I see it is that I've been cheated out of about thirty years."

Jesus's disappointment was so strong that Nicholas could feel its energy.

"Jesus, I say this with the utmost respect. I think the Father is all-merciful, and because I think this way, I don't have any fear of him. I mean, I just don't know why you or he would want me to have any greater faith than I have now. I believe in you, and I believe in God the Father. I just don't believe that everything will be okay after Aaron gets hit in the head by a puck."

He was getting a greater confidence, knowing that Jesus was listening to him and that he wasn't being struck down dead because of what he was saying. So, he let it all hang out now. "I know that you tested Abraham, and Francis has told me this is similar, by asking him to kill his son as a sacrifice to the Father. And I know that at the last second you held his hand from sticking the knife into his son's heart. But I am not Abraham. He was special, someone being schooled by you to help save his people. I am not Abraham. I am just a guy struggling to wake up each day and glad to find himself alive again. I am not a savior of the people of Astoria. I am no one special. You have never deemed me worthy to talk with me before.

"I know that you know the truth that is in each of us, so why don't I just face it with you. I'm talking all this intellectual stuff, and I'm covering up what's really going on in me. I'm afraid. That's it, I'm just afraid. Afraid for Aaron, my son, that if I say yes to your offer that he might die. And then where would I be?

"You know that I couldn't even have faith in the relic they put on my head early on in my cancer. Let's face it: I don't know *how* to have faith."

Finally, Jesus smiled.

"That's just it, Nicholas. No one knows *how* to have faith. You just do it. You make a leap in your heart and just do it. There isn't any magical way. Mother Teresa was asking me for a sign of her faith for over fifty years, and she did not receive one. Yet, she had faith, a very powerful faith. And why? Because she said so. It's as simple as that."

"I'm sorry, Jesus, but if it's as simple as that, then why would I have to put Aaron at risk? I'm really sorry. I'd like to do as you ask, but it just doesn't make sense to me. If Aaron must take a puck in the head for me to prove that I believe, then ... well, it just doesn't make any sense to me. I'm sorry, but you'll have to count me out."

It was a sad day for Jesus. Perhaps the human race had outgrown its need for faith. Though tempted to take upon himself the Godhead of his father, he decided to keep his promise to remain human.

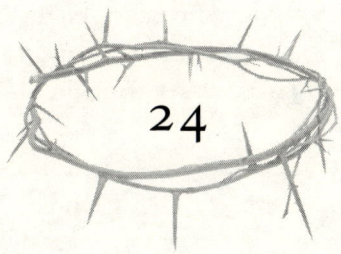

24

Francis had tried, but he had never been a salesman. He had never been able to enroll anyone in anything he didn't totally believe in himself. Once, when he was a young man, he took a summer job selling eating utensils, mostly knives, door to door in the Bronx. He found the whole thing rather silly, wondering why, if anyone wanted a large, sharp knife, why he didn't just go to the store and buy one. He was given a brief lesson in how to get entry into apartments after ringing the doorbell. If a man answered, he was told to say, "Can I talk to the missus?"

When he rang the bell of his first possible customer, an overweight and almost nude hairy-chested man answered the door. "Can I talk to the missus?" Francis dutifully asked. With that, the man bellowed, "There ain't no missus here," and slammed the door in his face. He never again tried to convince anyone.

When he finished delivering the mail and had done his best trying to convey to Tina, Richard, Bill, Cora, and Nicholas Jesus's intentions to offer them the gift of faith, Jesus was sitting in the blue chair, waiting for him.

"It hasn't been a good day," Nicholas said.

"I know," a dejected Jesus responded.

"Maybe I'm not the right guy to do this work." The ease he had been establishing in the presence of the Son of God was beginning to evaporate. Once again, he began to feel overwhelmed that he was in the presence of the Almighty. He was beginning to wish that he had not been favored.

"I have failed you."

He was shocked when Jesus said, "Yes, you have."

It was as if every fear he had as a child was now present, each piled on top of the other, each reinforcing the other. He was plain scared at Jesus's abruptness.

"How about you, Francis? You have shown very little interest in taking Thomas to the game, very little interest in the gift I am ready to offer you."

The sadness and disappointment began to get the better of Jesus. He put down his head and sobbed. It was almost imperceptible, yet evident to Francis. He wanted to go over to him and put his hand on his shoulder to console him. He thought a little about how he had once told Jesus in prayer that he would have carried the cross for him, but now he just couldn't get himself to cross the room. It wasn't that he didn't want to. He simply didn't know what to do. He was ashamed of his failure.

Strangely, shame had always been a source of strength to Francis. So, when Jesus raised his head to ask the inevitable, Francis was ready.

"I am sorry, Jesus, I will not be taking Thomas to the game." He thought for a second that Jesus might just disappear, poof, the way he had seen him do. That he would go out of his life and never come back again, that all the events of the past week would seem like a dream to him. Or, perhaps he wouldn't remember anything. After all, Jesus had told him at the outset that he might erase some of this from his and the others' memories.

"It's not that I don't believe in you, or what you have done here, that you have come to my home and have spoken to me. I feel like the most honored and privileged human being on the earth. It's just that I have mostly been an awful father to Thomas and Kyle. I want to be a better father, and somehow I think that taking Thomas to the game might not be so loving. I know that I'm not an Abraham. I have said this to you." He sensed that he was starting to speak like Jesus, but he didn't like it. He was beginning to feel more like Judas.

"Jesus! It's not easy to be human! I mean, sometimes I feel more drawn to bad things than I do to the good. Sometimes, I think that a force is pulling me toward chaos, and that I like going there. It's sort of an easier place to be. You know? Everything out of control makes life less hard. I can just blame things on others. When I'm in this place, it's all someone else's fault. I have nothing to do with it because I think I

can't do anything about anything. Then I'm on a sort
of easy street that I'm not responsible for anything."
He lowered his head before saying, "I'm sorry."

Neither Francis nor Jesus realized it, but the
strangest interlude was taking place. They both sat as if
thinking, perhaps trying to formulate something, anything, to push them forward to a more acceptable place.

"Do you want something to eat, Jesus?"

"No," he responded. And then he said, "Francis, I
think that you are a lazy man."

The shock on Francis's face was as pronounced as
it was evident.

"You are not lazy in the physical sense. But you are
lazy in what I'll call the moral sense. You have your
faults, you sometimes sin, yet I do not think you are a
sinner, a person who throws up his depravity into the
Father's face and does not care.

"But you are otherwise lazy. You find excuses,
reasons without merit, to denigrate your wife so that
you can get out of being a husband and a father. You
talk well about how you love your children, yet you do
little to show them that you do. You do not care about
your fellow workers at the post office. Do you not
know that they have each been put into your life for
a reason? That they are the co-workers given to you
in part to work out your salvation? They are special,
and you have never seen that. In fact, your attitude is
worse than not caring. You are indifferent."

He stopped and stared at Francis, as if expecting
an answer.

"I don't know what to say to you. I didn't realize it was so bad, I mean that I am so bad."

"I only want you to say that you will accept the gift of great faith that the Father is offering to you. I only want you to say that you agree to take Thomas to the game."

It is said that at some point in each of our lives that we will be faced with a great decision, one that might affect the rest of our lives, our destiny. Now was the moment for Francis. He could say yes to Jesus, or he could be honest with himself and say no.

"I am so sorry that I must say no to you. It grieves me because somewhere inside you I know that you are hurting. You have told me as much.

"Yet, I cannot bring myself to accept that everything will be okay, even if Thomas should die. I know what you are saying to me, but the only thing I know is this life, Thomas, things that are around me. And, frankly, Jesus, my friend..." Francis felt so much love for Jesus at that moment. He was disappointing him, something he did not want to do. The Son of God had made it so clear to him on several occasions that he knew what it is to be a man, with all the terror, anger, and love that comes with it. So, Francis knew how sad another disappointment could be.

It was at that very moment that Francis realized how powerfully his love for this man had been growing, that he had stopped seeing him just as the Son of God. It had happened only once or twice in Francis's life, but he did know how it felt to love a friend. He thought his heart might explode because he had disappointed Jesus so.

"Jesus, dear Son of God and my friend, I am going to tell you why I cannot take Thomas to the game. I've tried to tell you, but I think I have failed in the attempt. I will not take my son to the game because I do not see the purpose of it. I mean, I do not see why you want to test my faith, that you say to me, *Take Thomas to the game where he might be killed, but everything will be okay, even if he is killed.*

"I only know that things will be okay if I do *not* take him to the game. And I don't understand why you want to test me. I don't understand why we must have faith in what is not seen.

"Please, please, try to understand me." Knowing the awkwardness of the request, he went on. "It seems utterly unfathomable to me why you would want to test me, or anyone, for that matter. If you would only show yourself to everyone, as you have to me, I think we might all love you much more than we do. It is hard to love a shadow, to love the mist. If you only became real to us, we could know you. I think…" He wanted to soften things a bit by adding the word *perhaps*. "Perhaps we can only love someone that we know. Most of us do not know you. Even when we ask, we are not answered.

"I know that you love each of us, and I know also that you love me because you have been with me in this life that I know. You have acted lovingly toward me. Except, may I say without incurring your wrath, when you told me that I am a lazy man. I did not like that.

"It is because I know that you love me that I can be open to you, that I am right now expressing the fullness of my thoughts. I want to tell you that I am also afraid of you, afraid of the Father, because you might interpret that I am saying 'no' to your offer as disobedience. Am I to be condemned because I love my son? Am I to be thrown into the fires of hell because I do not understand, because I see the request as unfair, really, to me, as totally not understandable? I hope not."

Francis began to feel overcome by his honesty in the presence of God. He looked up at Jesus, tears in his eyes, and said, "If you are that kind of a God, I do not want to humble myself to you. I do not want to be with a God who is small and needy about things like ... like the hockey game request."

Francis could feel himself getting scared at what he had just revealed to Jesus. *What if I am wrong?* he thought. *What if God is really the way people thought he was a long time ago when they made sacrifices to him so that the crops might grow? What if he is the threatening and punishing God of the Old Testament?*

If he is, he thought, *I am in for it, big time.*

He was very aware that Jesus had lately seemed critical of Francis's clients, even a bit tired of them all. Certainly, now he must be fatigued with him, whom Jesus counted on to deliver the mail, to be a channel of his grace.

"Please, Jesus, do not be angry with me. I think the only reality that would have me take Thomas to the game is if you threatened to punish me. I'd like to say respectfully that I don't think you're that way. I hope you are not."

He got more scared when a distracted Jesus did not answer him.

"Did you say something to me, Francis?" he asked. "I've been talking to my Father about all of this."

"Jesus, I was saying to you that I believe you are a loving savior. I didn't say this, but I'm not so sure of the Father."

"Did I not tell you, Francis, that the Father and I are one?"

Francis was beginning to feel more ashamed of himself, and he started to think about his lack of faith in Jesus, who told him that everything would be okay at the hockey game, no matter what. But then he felt a host of reasons to continue to say no. He could not unglue himself from his past, could not free himself into the possibilities of the future.

"Jesus, the puck and the game, these seem just like the kind of stuff I know from ... it all seems ... " He stopped, thinking an excuse must be established for him to say what was on his mind. "It seems like the kind of thing my parents would do. You know, set me up for kicks, then whamoo. Like a sick thing."

"I am not your parents."

"But, you say 'the Father' so many times. I was not a good father. My father was not a good father."

"We are not like your father, of that I can assure you."

Francis had more to say. "You know that I'm generally an angry guy. I even get mad at pigeons in the park. I was mad at Ellen half the time in our marriage and most of the time I didn't even know why. I expect rejection."

"Francis, you have the capacity to be a man of great faith. And Thomas could be the catalyst to bring you there." He paused, and asked, "Do you want that?"

"I'm sorry, Jesus, but I do not."

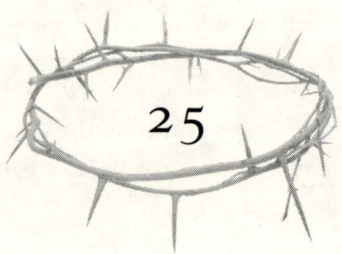

25

These words were to bring a great silence between the two, the quiet of a canyon floor after a landslide had run its rocky course. In Francis's mind, he had just perpetrated a great offense. He didn't think of it as a sin. In fact, he didn't think of it as having anything to do with morality. It was, for him, a sort of spiritual crime. Perhaps it was because he had come to know Jesus and loved him that saying a great "*no*" to him was not in the order of the worst sin he had always thought he might commit. It was more like refusing an important request from a friend, like turning down a buddy who came to rely on him.

"I am so sorry, Jesus, for saying '*no*' to you." He could feel himself begin to tremble because of what he would like to say now. He was very aware that he was in the same room as Jesus, breathing in the exhaled breath of God himself. That Jesus, the Son of God, was inhaling the breath of a common mailman. It was a startling place to be.

"Jesus, my friend … please believe me when I say that you are my friend. I am very confused right now. I do love you as my friend, and I also know that you are my God."

At this, Jesus got up from the blue chair and began to come toward him, while raising his right hand. By childhood experience and the resultant habits inspired by his parochial school upbringing, Francis expected a lightning bolt to crash into his forehead.

There was nothing. Jesus sat down again and said, "I know what you are trying to say to me is difficult for you. I would like to bless you, as I am confident that you speak the truth to me. I know, and the Father knows, that faith and the truth are one. I know I am beginning to sound a bit formal.

"I see, too, that you are beginning to sound formal," Jesus said with a smile. "It's okay, sometimes I am meant to suffer."

As Jesus joked at himself, Francis began to feel lighter, as if he was being released to say what was on his mind now that laughter had freed his heart.

"It's only that I have been used to not saying what is in my heart. We are all like that, I think. When childhood leaves us, it takes with it the ability to speak the truth."

"I am sorry to interrupt you, Francis. It is rude of me. Yet, sometimes I cannot help myself. The teacher in me just pops out. What I want to say is that we do not lose our ability to speak the truth. We simply lose our courage. It's not hard to lose it, you know, to lose courage when having it might mean losing a friend, an opportunity, a job. I understand these things."

Francis just stared, not knowing when to begin again, until the rhythms of their friendship let him know. "What I want to say is that I think I know why I have been a failure at delivering your message, although I don't know yet what Mrs. Aldrich and Richard Darby have to say about your proposal, if I may call it that.

"I must take a breath, a deep breath, before I go on, as I am very nervous to say this to you. It is the truth of what I think."

Of course, Jesus knew Francis's thought, and he wished that this cup, too, might pass. What Francis would say had to do with the most difficult part of the Father's relationship with people of the Earth. It was about faith, the quality of soul most made fun of by skeptics who didn't realize that dependence on reason alone was also a kind of faith.

"Jesus, I think that asking us to take the children we love to a hockey game where they might be killed in order to show that we have faith seems pointless, even absurd, to us. I am not certain if they all think this way, but it appears to be so."

Jesus looked at him as if he was not distracted by his own prayer for guidance. The look on his face conveyed a certain confidence to Francis that what he had to say might be making some sense.

"When I say this to you, Jesus…" He stopped, and said, "May I call you my brother?" Jesus received

these words with a tenderness that Francis had sometimes seen in works of art.

"I would welcome that," he said.

"Then I will say it. Please know that I tremble in
using the word.

"My brother, Jesus, we simply do not have the
capacity to understand what you ask us to do. Our
minds are the sharp knives that cut us off from you.
How could it be that you could ask such a thing? And
why? Why would you have us risk our children to
show you that we believe? Could we not just say so?
Could we not just say *I believe?*"

With a deep sadness in his eyes, Jesus answered,
"You could."

Francis took the response as a kind of checkmate
intended to end the conversation, though he felt that
a brother would not summarily do that.

"Jesus, I would like to have a meeting tomorrow
morning with everyone. I am a bit frightened that,
since they do not know you as I do, that they might
be unwilling to attend if you are there. You know how
it can take time. I ask you, therefore … there I go
again … I'd like it if you were not there."

"That is good, Francis. I will not be there."

"Please, though, tell me more about why you are
making this request of us."

With a begging quality, he said again, "Please."

"I will tell you."

With what might be called pride that he, only he
of all earthlings, was about to know the mind of God,
Francis listened more carefully than he ever had.

"The Father has not been pleased with the progress of this planet. He created it in love, yet its people have not realized their potential to make it a place that works for everyone and everything. He added, "You even kill unborn babies."

"We, the Father and I, have met several times with our Spirit and the Council to discuss this, to see what we might do to help the situation." He stopped and with a certain look that Francis took to be disgust, he said in a voice that could hardly be heard, "Too many wars, too many leaders who aren't really leaders."

"How does this fit into the hockey game?"

"I will tell you, but not before I have a glass of orange juice, please. You might not believe me, but being human is not always easy for me."

Quickly, Francis got the orange juice, not so much to be polite as it was to get back to the revelations to come.

"Thank you, Francis. Now, let's continue. In order to help get the world back on track, we thought it would be useful to ask certain individuals if they would take upon themselves the risks to be people of great faith. In this way, they would become like bright beacons for others on the planet. Because people on earth can co-create the evolution of the human spirit with the Father, we thought this would be the beginning of a kind of phalanx of humans who might show the way to others.

"This is why I am disappointed in what has happened here in the past few days."

"I am sorry I have failed you," Francis said.

"It is not you who have failed. Ever since the Garden of Eden, you have all been failing yourselves."

And then he said the most fascinating thing.

"It took us time to realize that even the people I most respect are imperfect, that people are pulled to their weaknesses, that it takes a lot to overcome these imperfections. In some human way, I am beginning to lose my optimism. It is never that I and the Father have stopped loving you. If it ever could be said that the Father has a reason for being, it is to love you.

"Could it be," Francis asked Jesus, a perplexed look on his face, "that we are beginning to lose faith in you?"

Stunned by his own boldness in saying this to Jesus, Francis looked at him, thinking that God might strike him dumb.

What he saw was Jesus, his body slightly trembling in an ecstasy of love. He could see in Francis the possibilities of man as created by the Father.

"My dearly beloved brother," Jesus said in a voice that softly echoed love, "you have said it. You know, yet you do not know, that you are all losing faith in God. You have said it."

26

Before he tried to organize the meeting, Francis knew that he had to see Ellen about taking Thomas to the hockey game.

"Ellen, what I am about to tell you is startling, perhaps even unbelievable. For the past several days I have been in touch with a very special person. I hardly know how to say this, because what I am about to say is surreal. This special person is someone we have all heard about, sometime or another. Even those who don't believe in religion probably have heard of him." She kind of rolled her eyeballs, thinking that Francis was beginning to lose it.

"Let me just say who it is." Given their relation-ship, he knew she would take this for a joke. "I have been talking with Jesus Christ himself."

"You know, Francis," she said with a bubbling anger at this weird expression of what she thought her ex had become, "I know that you have a lot of issues with the church. I know you're twisted up inside yourself for who knows what, but making a joke about Jesus is something you'll be sorry for. You just can't kid around about stuff like that."

Francis knew that nothing he could say might convince her of the truth of his story. It was time for another minor miracle. "Oh, God," he said out loud.

Ellen had a medium-sized statue of the Blessed Mother holding the baby Jesus that sat on the bureau in what used to be their bedroom. It was a family heirloom, passed down for several generations and treated with such respect and care that not one of its gilded trimmings had been worn over the years. All of a sudden, the statue flew into the living room where they were sitting. It began to do a dizzy dance about four feet over Ellen's head. Faster and faster it went, until stopping on the coffee table before it turned itself upside down, now spinning like an ice skater at the end of her routine, but on her head. When it stopped, it fell over onto the glass top of the table, causing the baby Jesus to break off from its mother.

"Oh, God," Ellen shouted. Francis didn't know if the exclamation was prompted by the miraculous flight of the statue or its breakage. He was, though, pleased to know that the words worked only for him.

Trying to calm her, he said, "I'm sorry, Ellen, if this little miracle broke the statue. I was just trying to get you to realize that I am not joking about Jesus. He really does meet with me."

As Ellen began to scoop up the two pieces of the

porcelain statue, she looked at Francis with a measure of hatred in her eyes. "You know how special this is to me."

"Yes, I do," he said as he sat down and allowed her to gather her wits. "Are you ready now," he asked, "to hear my story?"

She simply threw up her arms in a gesture of resignation.

"I know this is a lot to take in. Imagine how I felt when it first happened to me. I thought it was a joke, too. For the past several days, I have been asked by Jesus to deliver letters to five families, my clients, in an apartment house in the neighborhood. The story is quite complicated, just about unbelievable. I've learned things about God, and things about Jesus's life that have blown me away. We don't have time right now for me to tell you about these things. Perhaps some day we'll have time."

"You know that you are taxing my imagination and my patience."

"Yes, yes, I do. But please hear me out. He's picked the five and me, I have to tell you, because he wants them, us, to be the forerunners of people who have a great faith in God, and faith that everything will eventually work out. He says that if we believe that everything will be all right, we will start to love each other in ways that we have not for a long time, that we will lose our selfishness. It sounds probable, at least to me, that if we think things will work out that we won't be so afraid of each other. He told me that each one of us can create with God, and with others, the

continuing growth of loving spirituality in the world."
He paused before saying to Ellen, "Don't you think?"
She just looked at him and did not answer.

"Now, here's the hard part. Jesus says that if I take
Thomas to the Rangers' game, remember, I promised
I'd take him? That I have to be willing to put Thomas
in a seat where a hard shot might hit him in the head
and kill him. But that if I believe everything will be
okay, then I can be one of the men of great faith."

Ellen looked at him as if he were nuts. "Let's see
if I've got this right. You take Thomas to the game
where he might get killed by a puck, and you get to be
a great man."

"Well, not exactly. Each of the persons he's picked
will do the same thing with their kid. They might
get hit and they might not. Don't worry, though. I've
already told Jesus that I wouldn't be taking Thomas to
the game. I just can't see the sense in it, and I've told
Jesus this, about an hour ago."

"Good for you," Ellen said. "Now, I know that you
have been hobnobbing with Jesus, but I've got to get
on with a few ordinary things, you know, like getting
dinner for the kids, making sure they do their homework, things like that."

The dismissal wasn't a hard pill for Francis to
swallow. His interest in revealing the information to
Ellen was simple: to get a few honeyed words from
her, a reward for refusing Jesus's offer to sacrifice
Thomas. As he was used to being unacknowledged by
her, it was just like old times.

"Well, it's good to see you, Ellen," he said politely. "I've got to get on."

"Yes," she said under her breath, "to do God's work, I'm sure."

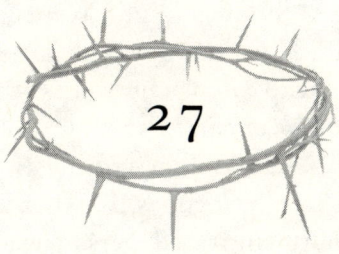

27

"Thank you all for coming to our apartment. It might have been a bit of a walk for some of you. So, I appreciate that you took the time to take the walk. We've got two different kinds of juices, some tiny donuts, an assortment of crackers and, and...please, we bought plastic cups." Using the plural seemed to take the self-awareness out of being alone.

Sitting on an extra large blue sofa were Bill Waxman, still trying to find forgiveness for killing so many of the enemy on Iwo Jima many years ago; Beverly, with her Nicholas seeking health and self-possession; and Cora, attempting to recover from disillusionment and profligate sex. Francis took the three chairs he had in the apartment and placed them so that they faced the sofa. He sat in the middle one, where he hoped to discover who he was. Tina, trying to recover from being abandoned by Joe, sat on his left. And Mr.

Darby, wanting a drink for his body and forgiveness
for his soul, sat on Francis's right. It was a cozy circle.

"Please, Mr. Mailman, stop the BS and let's get
on with it. I want to know why you asked us to come
here." It was Bill Waxman.

"Well, Bill … Mr. Waxman, I guess you're right.
We'll get right to it." At times like this, Francis, who
was not a socially cultivated person, was glad for a
Waxman who demanded that he cut right to the chase.

Nicholas was the only one who wanted to eat.
Sugar and spice seemed to be the only remaining fla-
vors his taste buds, so altered now by his treatment,
enjoyed in the time left to him. He went right for the
cookies, while the rest waited politely for him.

"In one way or another, I have spoken to each of
you in the past few days about Jesus and the hockey
game," Francis began. "That he would like each of you
to go to the game with your child. Each of you has
declined. He has even asked me to take my son, and I
too have said no.

"It's sad, in a way, that all of us have answered his
request like this. I am not going to try to convince
anyone here to change his or her mind. I'd just like
us to talk about it for a while. I'd like that because I
think, in our own unimportant way, that we have been
made important. What I mean to say is that if Jesus
himself has come here to speak with us that maybe,
just maybe, we *are* special."

He was not used to talking with others like this,
and he knew that he was in the middle of something
he did not understand. "In a very real way, I wish I

wasn't involved in this. I am not smart enough to be standing here, trying to make some sense. I think maybe Jesus picked the wrong guy."

Beverly knew how he felt, a person doubting himself. She knew how the few trips she had taken with sick Nicholas, and the many yet to come, had weakened her own spirit. How each note of optimism by one of his doctors was counterbalanced by a different one's discouraging innuendo in the uncoordinated mess called cancer treatment. Soon enough she was left with the distinct impression that it was all part of a self-protective game they played to pretend there was hope while keeping hold onto the grim reality.

From childhood, she wanted to believe in God's goodness. She was, though, unwilling to sacrifice her son to the desire. She now realized Nicholas's sudden and weird way of leaving her and the kids might have been prompted by the tumor. And, although she had tried to be her own woman since he left, she was still pulled toward a need to entrust herself to him. It was a reflex she did not like. The tug was lessening, yet she could still feel its pull.

"Perhaps, Mr. Mailman. No, no ... what is your name?" It was Waxman.

"His name is Francis," Mr. Darby blurted out.

"Perhaps, Francis, you are not the wrong guy for this job. Maybe you are precisely the right guy," Bill said, to everyone's surprise. Francis nodded, as if to say thank you.

Mr. Darby again spoke out. "Let me say that I think it's a damn funny place we're all in, here. I don't mean the room, I mean what's being asked of us. I know, speaking for myself, that I don't even find it decent to be asked to sacrifice little Erin. Even if I could do it, I don't have a lot of confidence in God right now. I told Francis that I would think it over. Well, I have." He paused, harrumped a bit, and said, "I'm not saying there's no God, but that's what I've got to say."

His way of speaking echoed like a sharp rebuke to the conversation and to the group. Francis was afraid it also might shut them down, that the meeting would be over before anyone had a chance to speak. "Before I forget," he said in an awkward way, "does anyone else have anything to say?"

The silence seemed forever to Francis. And then, as if he was on automatic, Mr. Darby shouted, "I have something to say. I want you all to know that I have been trying very hard since my wife died to not drink anymore. It has been several weeks. I've been told at the meetings I go to that people who are trying to stop after a long time of drinking too much are faced with a lot of difficulties trying to make amends for their past.

"Let's not pretend that you don't know that I was driving the car the day my wife died. I am trying to come to grips with that, even though I wasn't drinking that day. I am trying to find ways of speaking with her ... and I do that in prayer and with my daughter, who I think finds me ugly. I am trying to make it up to her. Erin, my daughter, that is. And I am full of shame and guilt.

"Lately, too, I have thought that my lack of faith in God is another way to punish myself. If I had faith in God ... maybe in life itself. Then I wouldn't have to punish myself so much. I would believe that if I asked for forgiveness that it would be given to me."

Suddenly, Cora Aldrich cut him off.

"Yes, yes, Mr. Darby, maybe that's what it means when it says that whenever we ask God anything in the name of Jesus that it will be given to us. Maybe it means that when we ask something that's good, something that Jesus would agree with, then we'll get what we ask for.

"Of course it means that. So, when you ask him to forgive you for your wife's death, for drinking too much, then he will. It makes sense because I think Jesus wants to forgive. Maybe that's who he is, a forgiving God."

She sat down and stared at the wall behind the three chairs. It was as if she was amazed at herself, and in the wonder, suddenly fell on her knees. The eyes of the others began to widen, some in fear that the meeting might be turning into a wild and unruly affair, others in fear that they, too, might be called on to demonstrate how they felt about these things.

"Oh, God," she uttered, "forgive me, please, for being unfaithful to my husband in so many ways and with so many men, including a person in this room." Each one in the room began to look at the other, wondering who that person might be. Preoccupation with themselves and the accompanying ruminations about each other had become so heightened by now that they even looked at Tina Remsen. Maybe she was included in the possibilities. Who knows to what extent a slut might go, they thought.

Compassion with Cora did not live in the room. Its guests and Francis were more engrossed in judgments about how she had broken the code of not speaking about these things in public. "Do you really think, Mrs. Aldrich, that we want to hear about the things you have done?" It was Tina, a self-conscious Tina who more and more lately, in her longing for the love of her indifferent husband, had taken upon herself a disproportionate and imaginative sense that she was capable of committing shameful sins. If Cora was the way she was, then she could be that way too.

Sensing the tension building, Francis broke in. "Perhaps we should all take a break, and get a cookie … or two," he added.

They welcomed the opportunity and did as he suggested. The exchange of pleasantries, important as they were, was forced. Saying what they were really thinking was out of the question. Secret things were already leaking out. Behavior could get primitive under these circumstances, as there seemed to be so much at stake for each of them. After all, saying no to Jesus might have consequences that none of them wanted.

With the assistance of a cane, Nicholas walked over to Cora. He smiled before asking her if he could get her a cookie. Would that it was as simple as that. What he said to her was, "A nookie for a cookie?"

"Why, you little creep," she yelled. "I ought to take

that cookie and shove it down your throat." He looked at her and smiled before Francis moved to separate the two.

"He has a cancer in his brain," he reprimanded Cora. "Try to understand." Although he said this in a whisper as thin as the hissing noise made by a little snake, his words were brusque and taken as a signal for the others to release the pent-up anger, so far held in check by fear.

"I can tell that you're all looking at me," Tina said, "like I'm the one she referred to as the other person in the room who she … who she did it with. I know I have a jerk for a husband, a guy who doesn't know up from down, but I'm not one of those."

Munching on cookies, the others looked at her, really not very interested in what she had to say. Even though some of them thought she might be the other person, they were interested only in the juiciness of the possibility that someone was not who they seemed to be, a heterosexual person. As if that was critical, as if that was something you announced when you were introduced: "I'd like to introduce you to my fellow heterosexual, Mrs. Remsen," or "I'm Mrs. Remsen, and I'm a heterosexual."

Cora came to her defense. "She's not the other person. What do you think I am, a dyke or something? It's a guy." Of course, this would set off another round of speculation, a safer kind now, though, as no guy would likely stand up to take the hit.

"Let me tell you all something else," Cora continued. "Sure, I want to be forgiven for my sins. But, I'm not some kind of apple polisher. I'm not going to say yes to anyone who puts my Angelina in jeopardy. I'm not going to take her to that hockey game. No way."

"Maybe we could all sit down again," Francis said. "I don't know if anyone has anything new to say, anything different I can take back to Jesus."

"You tell Jesus," Mr. Waxman said, "that I think he's not being very fair to us at all. I talk to him all the time. He never talks back. Tell him for me, Francis, that I'd like to hear from him once in a while."

"And you tell him for me," chimed in Nicholas, "you tell him for me that I'm only forty..." He began to stammer. "Only forty years old, and I'm dying. You tell him that I don't think it's fair. Why should I die so young? You tell him it's not fair. I've asked his Father in his name to make me better, and it's not happening, not gonna happen. It's just not fair. You tell him."

"You can be certain I will," said Francis, knowing that Jesus already knew.

Without being asked, they each felt it was time to vent their grievances.

"Please tell Jesus I love him," Cora said. "Tell him that I want to find the light. But tell him that the only thing I know now that is true for me, the only person who shows me the light is my daughter. Tell him he asks for too much. That I am a weak woman who is trying to be strong. Tell him that sacrificing my daughter is not the way for me to get strong. Ask him, please, to ask me to say yes to something that I can handle. I just can't handle this one. Tell him I'm sorry."

"I will tell him," Francis answered dutifully.

Mr. Darby stood up and walked to one side of the group so that each person could see him. Again, he spoke with the kind of gusto that sometimes accompanies personal whining. "I don't know why I have been afflicted with alcoholism. I sometimes wonder why me. Ask Jesus why he picked me to be this way. Why me? Ask him why so many rotten things have happened to me. Why is it just when I'm trying, really trying, to help out my wife that she gets killed in a car that I'm driving. She didn't even want me to go with her that day, said she'd do it alone. But I insisted, and now she's dead.

"Ask him why I had such lousy parents. And while you're at it, tell him, just tell him, that I'd like to have faith in him. And let him know why I would. Because maybe it would help me get through the day. Ask him to give me faith so I could get through the day. Ask him to do something, anything, for me. Tell him I don't know where he is. Tell him mostly that I'm afraid of lots of things, that I know that fear runs me, but I'm not afraid of him. You know, tell him that I really don't see him as a God who punishes. I just don't think that's him."

The room was quiet. Richard went back to his seat, covered his face with his hands, and sobbed. Only Tina came to his side to comfort him. And then, prompted by the candid ways of the others, she spoke her mind. "Francis, I want to thank you for being a messenger of God. You know, it's like being an angel. I have no idea why I am involved in this. In fact, it troubles me that I don't have the answer to that question. Sometimes, I think that God has his favorites, and I wonder why. I guess it's not for me to say. But I do wonder.

"It's nice to be on the good end of that, as I guess everyone here is. You know, he's offering us a special gift. Why us? Why me? I've never done anything special in my life. I'm a librarian. I help people get books, use the computers, send them on their way. Happy, I suppose. At least I try to send them home happy, especially the children.

"I read the Bible. I've even read the Old Testament. I know the story of Abraham and Isaac. Please tell Jesus that I'm no Abraham. I'm just a lady trying to stand on my own feet and love my son, Christopher, at the same time.

"Do you know where the name Christopher comes from?" she asked no one in particular. "It comes from a story … I don't know if it's true … about a boy who helped people cross a small fjord by carrying them on his back. One day a big man asked to be carried. The boy nearly drowned but got the man across. When they got to the other side, the man said to him, 'I am Jesus. From now on you will be called "Christopher," the one who carries Christ.'"

Not one to show her emotions, she stopped to regain her composure, before saying, "That is my son. I love him as I would like to love Christ."

Just then old Mr. Waxman blurted out, "Since we've all said no to Jesus, and we've already bought the tickets to the game, some of us would like to know, and here's where you come in, Francis, if it's going to be safe for us to still go to the game. You know, without anything happening."

"I don't know. But I can ask."

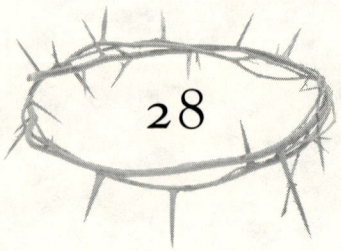

28

Francis asked Jesus if they could meet. He could now do this by simply thinking the thoughts, and he would be heard. "Though I need to be alone for awhile," he added.

As he walked through the streets of Astoria with all its hustle and bustle, he felt as if he was walking on waves of clarity where it all made sense, then on darkness where all was a puzzle. Here he was, in the middle of something profound. Yet, whatever happened might be erased in less than a flash of God's desire. No memory. No reality. He wondered if this week really happened if Jesus chose to blot it out.

His neighborhood was a little representation of the world, and probably had all the dramas of the world going on in it. Greeks, Hispanics, Italians, Irish, Chinese. A little bit of everyone. Music blaring, taxis honking, vendors hawking. Dogs walking shilly-shally. Zig-zag drunks. Newspapers on the stands of kiosks and shops, poking his eyes with headlines—the world a bit frantic. No one saying hello, no one nodding the existence of the other. The underskin of all this could be different. It was all there, the is and the what ought to be. Somehow, he was in the middle of it all.

"Jesus, I know you know this, but please allow me to say it to you. I don't know how else to handle it. You know what I think, what the group thinks, but I and they don't know what you are thinking."

"Yes," is all he said.

"You seem to be down," Francis said to him. "I think I am starting to understand what you mean when you've told me about taking on human flesh so that you would know."

"Yes. It is not easy, especially when the Father—I have such high expectations for you all."

"I hope you understand what I'm about to say, but I thank you for being human. I am grateful that you understand." Immediately, he wanted to take it back, fearing that Jesus might think that he was happy that the Son of God was suffering. "I didn't mean," was all he got out before Jesus said, "I understand. I appreciate what you have just said. I know what you meant."

It took a minute for this intimacy to sink in and for them to regain the equilibrium to proceed.

"I guess you know that they all said no. And you know that I also said no to the offer of your gift. I'm sorry. I guess we don't really know what faith is. For most of us it's a sort of reflex, a place we go to when there are no answers. Like a default when we don't know what to do, when we might go crazy with the mystery of it all.

"They've asked me to ask you a question about the hockey game. It's just that none of them is rich, and they paid hard-earned money for the tickets. They want to know if they can bring their children to the game. That nothing will happen. That you know how they feel, that you will not punish their children if they go."

"I will be busy for a bit. I must talk with the Father and with the Council. Please go."

The Father spoke first.

"My beloved Son sits at my right side. The Spirit is here. I have asked you to gather so we can talk.

"But first I want to say how good it is to be with you. I am always with you, but today in a different way because I am with you in the Spirit of my Son, who is in the flesh. I have chosen to be this way today, and I know you might think it manifests a weakness in me, that I experience the frailty of man only through my Son. In ways not comprehensible, I know what is in every creature, just as I count the hairs on every head. I know that each of you on the Heavenly Council has this knowledge of me, that you have believed.

"I know, too, that if my much loved people on Earth could picture this meeting, if we appeared on YouTube this day, many of them would still not believe. They are so easily deceived, so many times manipulated that they do not believe. Even if they believed that they were truly seeing us, some would not accept the mystery that my Son, I, and the Spirit are one. They would use what I have said about experiencing the flesh through my Son as a loophole to not believe in the possibility of saying yes to the spiritual gifts offered. They would say I am incomplete. They are so inclined, I must say by nature, to believe only what is in their experiences.

"I know from the indwelling of my Son that I am growing weary. When I am in the flesh of him, I conceive in my mind, without conceiving, that I am what you might call world-weary.

"Let us proceed. I want to say again how pleased I am to be with you now. Albert, my dear friend. Thank you for bringing our beloved animals to their joy again. When they are re-united with their humans, you will be fulfilled in the Spirit.

"And Dag, you are my voice on earth. You bring my Spirit to so many who try to govern the world. So many, too many, do not hear my voice. It is but a faint echo in the dark side. Yet, you try, you try. In my own way, I am in your debt.

"My dear Diana, how the children love you. How I love you that you continue to give the beauty of your nurturing spirit to them as they regain the completeness of their birthright. They are in your debt.

"Let me first say hello to Arland, who is the wonder of us all. No greater gift can be given than what

you have chosen to give. You continue to give the ultimate in you, a startling manifestation of selflessness.
Arland, you are the best of mankind. You are what I
intended humans to be. I am grateful that you always
said yes to the gifts offered, even on that icy cold day
in the Potomac River.

"Juan, whenever I see the unsatisfactory results of
what creatures can be, I think of you and your goodness. How joyful I am when I think of you.

"And Jimmy, I know that I have chosen to speak
with you last, for the last shall be first. Unlike Arland,
who gave himself to the ice for others, you gave yourself to fire for others. Whenever I think of what you
mean to me and to my message, I cry tears of joy. I
know that humans sometimes like to say that they
are grateful from the depth of who they are. I am the
depth of who I am. Thank you for being who you are."

They each fell on their knees before the God of
their fathers in what was an inexpressible desire to pay
homage. Each was blessed with a great awareness that
they were in the ineffable presence of goodness. In
their exalted condition, they were now beyond motiva-
tion, beyond fear, beyond love as an act of the will. In
knowing the love of the Father for every person, they
were necessarily, as a law of nature prevails, drawn to
him and to the essence of he who is. This was done
without expectations. The joy was in the homage, an
ecstasy never experienced before except, perhaps, in
very brief flashes when all seemed perfect on a day.

"You know that my Son has been to earth, where
he has asked Francis the mailman to convey his good

wishes and the offering of the gift of faith to certain families who live in a part of New York called Astoria. These are hard-working and good people, the salt of the earth.

"The mission, as you know, was planned as a mild kind of intervention to help the clumsy efforts of the people, in a non-interfering way, to accept the gift of an extraordinary faith. We are, as you know, upset with the conduct of many of our creatures.

"For a long time, I was thought of as an avenging God, a God of death. Very harsh thoughts about me were written in the First Books. Most all of them were simply projections of man's imagination. In the slow growth of man's ways of loving, he ascribed to me the anger and wrath he felt toward his own fellows."

What he said next surprised the Council members.

"Sometimes I want to be the God of the Old Testament. I know that an intention of mine can vaporize the earth. I resist, though I am more than annoyed at their conduct."

Without being asked, in the unity of perfect harmony, Jesus spoke.

"Thank you, our Father, my Father. As I am one with you and with the Spirit, I know of your anger. I can feel it in my body, and like a baby in the womb of his mother absorbs the love of his mother's body, I am of you. In oneness, you and I are. We abide, each in the essence of the other.

"Each of you, my dear friends, through the grace of our Father, continues to grow in this way, the ever-expanding joy of your identity strengthened within the essence of our Father's love. You are here because you have said yes to the gifts offered. As time has gone by and humans have progressed in their achievements and in their power over things of the earth, it has been more difficult for most to say yes. They are so caught up in the frivolous, the empty.

"Each of the five, as well as Francis, has said no. We have come to you today to ask for advice regarding what to do. We could end what I call 'the mission' and leave no recollection of what has transpired. We could show our wrath by having the mission in a tragedy—"

Princess Diana rose before Jesus finished. "With humility, I interrupt. If you were to do that, I will no longer want to be here in this place called heaven. It would no longer be the place where love rules. I say this while trembling before you. It's just that the people on earth are reflections of the goodness that can be. If you were to kill just one of them," she said in the most formal way before hesitating. "It is a sign of disappointment and uncontrolled anger, to absolutely kill possibility. Love will never prevail." She put her head down before saying, "It is what I think."

Ordinarily, Jesus would say to words like these that he understood, that he knew the love. Not responding in the usual way struck the members of the Council as being foreboding. Diana, always extra-sensitive, dared to ask him if he understood what she meant.

"I understand," he answered. "Let us get back to the negative answers. Besides having them all forget what has happened, or knowing that vengeance is mine, we could let them remember that they have disappointed the Father. We could let them always think of what has happened and allow them to tell others how they refused to accept the gift of faith. Perhaps this will quicken the world to complete the vision of my Father. It is a way to let the world know from the first-hand evidence of those who have said '*no.*'

"There are, of course, other ways. The Father and I in the Spirit could just give up on humans. We could simply abandon those on earth and allow things to go continually toward an inevitable disaster. If humans do not see that they can co-create the world along with us, we can withdraw our offers and let them simply die off. You know, the earth will warm, things will change, subjects will allow the powerful to make false promises, and misusing resources will escalate. In time, the earth and all in it, people, animals, trees, plants, water, everything, will dry up. And then it will be no more." The images Jesus drew of a world gone dry was stunning for the members of the Council. It was Juan Ramirez, with tears in his eyes, who asked to be heard. Jesus loved him so fully that he always welcomed hearing from him, for he knew his soul was inextricably bound with insight and truth.

"Lord Jesus, my brother, my friend, my God. How I love to be in your presence. It has been my gift always to try to say yes to you. I don't know why I do that. It is as if I cannot do anything else. It pleases me to do what you ask.

"But today when you speak of the blood that will dry up, I cannot think something different in my heart, something I have not yet ever thought. How is it that I can go against you, my friend, my God? I see my people suffer in the history. I know they suffer now. I bleed in my soul for the blood in their bodies. I see the babies, and I know how beautiful they are. I know the future can be good.

"So I will say it to you. I do not like when you speak that you and the Father have the power to abandon them. I call upon the greatness of my people's humble resolve to say to you that you must never abandon the people of the earth. Please, Jesus, hear the words in my love." Always respectful, he ended by saying, "Thank you."

Arland Williams was used to offering lifesavers, so he did what he knew best: he threw Jesus a lifesaver, as weird as he considered the thought to be. "Jesus, please allow me to speak."

"It is why you are here," Jesus answered.

"If you had not come to earth two thousand years ago, you might not speak the way you have just spoken. You would not have known people as they really are. Sometimes we are dumb, foolish, unenlightened, mean-spirited. Too often, we are cruel.

"I cannot explain to you how grateful I am for the privilege you have given to me to express myself here today. What lives in my heart is the way I remember people on the day I died. In the year before that afternoon, I began to see everyone with a different pair of eyes from the way I had seen them for my entire life.

"You know, Jesus, that I was an ordinary kind of guy. But I was always trying to be better, always learning more about myself and others. I began to notice that I was listening more to everyone. They all began to seem valuable to me, even the ones who talked so much, the ones I used to put down in my head because I thought they didn't care about others. When I finally began to listen to their stories, I realized that they had important things to say. I think I began to understand that each of them was somebody."

He thought that Jesus was looking at him askance. "I know that you already know what I am about to say. Please, though, allow me to say it, for my sake. Just for my sake, please, because if I do not, I will think that I have failed in my own vision. To each you have given an intellect, to many a vision. I hope my own is a reflection of the Father's. That day when I offered my lifesaver to others, I loved them. I truly did. I think that I said yes to the offer to love. I knew they must have had faults. Don't we all? Maybe they weren't people of great faith. I don't really know. What I was certain of, though, was that they deserved to be loved. And I had the chance to do that. To love them.

"It wasn't easy. You know that. The water was very cold and it was very cold outside. I think I knew that it was over for me. My legs were trapped in the jagged metal. I couldn't feel them anymore. I didn't think I could get out. If I'd have taken one of the life jackets thrown to me, I probably would have just frozen to death anyway. I was always a practical guy. Ask my wife. She'd tell you. It was all surreal, you know, the noise from the choppers, people yelling to each other, the faces of a few around me in the water, so filled with terror. Really, I just had to help them. It wasn't any big deal."

Bound in a spiritual tie with his Son, a bond not understandable, yet somehow grounded in the humanity of Jesus, the Father's eyes grew moist as he listened to Arland, before a single teardrop, divine in its essence, human in its expression, ran down his cheek. For a brief moment, the Council members became present to the fullness of their own divinely inspired capacity to love. Like a dropped stone answering to the call of gravity, they loved him.

All the while, Dag listened. What he was hearing frightened him, because it sounded as if the Father's disappointment in humans might be shifting him to do something terrible. Could it be a foreboding of the long-expected apocalypse? Jimmy, too, was frightened, just like he was the night of the fire.

29

"Francis, I want you to know that the meeting of the Heavenly Council did not go all that well. My Father is somewhat angry about the behavior of earth's people. He created the earth as a place in time that might evolve into a kind of forerunner, a place to prepare its people for the paradise to come. When first he was deeply disappointed in what you were making of yourselves, he sent a man named John to baptize, to prepare everyone for my coming. None of you ever did see that John was the precursor to my coming in the same way that this earth was to be the precursor to the kingdom of heaven.

"Yet, you have made a mess of things. You have polluted the rivers of the earth, scorched the land, disrespected its animals, defiled each other by killing. Do you know how disappointed we are whenever there is a war? I say *we* because I speak of the Father in whom I dwell. When I am sad, he is also.

"We see how you slay each other in war. How you sink to the lowest form of human behavior when you kill each other, when you refuse to use the gifts of intellect and tongues to talk rather than to kill. How you take your young men and women, impressionable, seeking adventure, and train them each to kill. At least when the animals on the plains of Africa kill..."

Suddenly, he stopped, as if the things he was talking about brought to him a divine sadness that no person could ever comprehend.

"I'm so sorry," Francis whispered. "What do you intend to do?"

"I'm not sure," he answered tersely, "but I am sad with the grief of love."

"Jesus, I know this is not a good time to bring this up again. It seems so mundane.

But what about the game? Can they go to the game without any of the children getting hurt?"

"I think so. But right now I am not certain. It is not a good time."

By now, Francis had begun to assume the role of a go-between. He found this sort of comical, a twist on the reality of the way things had been in the past. Here he was, trying to solve the tensions that existed between his own customers and Jesus, the bridge between what is and what ought to be.

"I think there might be a way. Mr. Darby has asked me to tell you that he is willing to take the hit for everyone, if it means that they will all, each of them, have an increase in their faith. He just doesn't want Erin to be there when it happens. She's had a lot to deal with, you know."

"Of course, I know. Mr. Darby is the last man we'd want to be sacrificed at the game. He hates himself, and he doesn't believe in anything. Never has."

"But, isn't this different?" Francis interrupted. "If he says that he will die for the others, then he must believe in what you are offering, he must believe in your word."

"I don't think he really believes, though what you say has some merit. Perhaps someday he will come around to thinking about something other than himself. Right now he thinks that he must be punished for his drinking and the death of his wife. He hasn't asked for forgiveness, nor has it entered into his mind to ask." When Jesus stopped, he flung his arms in the air in a gesture of frustration. Looking at Francis, he said, "You really don't know how it works, do you?"

"I'm sorry," the mailman answered, "but I don't know what you mean."

"I mean that before the impulse to ask for forgiveness even sparks in a man's heart, the Father and I through the Spirit have already forgiven him. One might say that we exist to love, we live to forgive.

"And yet, Richard has not even thought about forgiveness. He is so taken up with himself, so consumed by his need to control everything, that he thinks that he alone can make faith and forgiveness happen. He has not yet realized that he must work with us, with others in the spirit of the universe, to make it happen. Perhaps in offering grace and faith at the hockey game, we are offering this understanding."

"I think," Francis answered, "that what you say is beyond our understanding. Please know that Mr. Darby is ready to be sacrificed. If you, the Father, change your mind, he is ready. He will be your Abraham. But there will be no Isaac."

Francis had no idea where his courage came from. Perhaps it was an impulse, like the impulse a man in battle gets to save another, an urge to answer for some greater good yet not explainable so that it would make much sense. If a man can be drawn to the banality of evil without thinking, maybe he can be pulled to the inspiration of goodness just as unwittingly.

Francis said in an unusually firm voice, "Please forgive me, but I have an opinion."

"Explain yourself, Francis."

"Jesus, please don't be angry at me, but I'm going to say it. As it is for me, at least." He thought about stopping to get a drink of water, go to the bathroom, anything he could think of to break the tension he was feeling. He realized, though, that if he stopped, that he might not ever have the nerve to say these things again.

"I know that my thinking is limited, but I think what you are asking them to do is not fair. You are asking them to sacrifice what is most dear to them, their children, and with no guarantees except your word that all will be okay no matter what happens, even if their child is killed instantly by a hockey puck."

"My dear friend, Francis, faith means there is no

guarantee, just an acceptance that in the end all will be fine."

"That's all well and good for you to say. You're God and you know how it's all going to play out. You know the ending of everything. We don't. We can't. We're not you.

"I can only speak for myself," Francis continued. "It is as if, in some respects, I am nothing. I am not reliable. I'm just not there when I'm supposed to be, you know, with the kids and all. But, I am trying to connect with you, who is everything. In the nothingness of me, I am looking for the allness of you. There is some deep disorder in me, and it lives in my core. Sometimes, I think I am a slave to it.

Francis thought if he was going to be punished for his thoughts, he might as well get as many of them on the table as he could before the bolt of lightning hit him right smack in the middle of his brain. Jesus interrupted the riff.

"Maybe not having faith is a way that you have of negating yourself, a way of not accepting that the countless exercises of your worst selves can be forgiven. Maybe it's a way to be always in a state of not knowing."

"You talk about not knowing as if it was something that we like, but it seems as if you and the Father have created this world so that we don't know, can't know. I think that even those among us who say that faith is the acceptance of a child are unsophisticated in their own way. Relying on our intellects alone is a kind of faith, a belief that what we conclude with our minds is the truth. How can we really be certain?

"I have read about so many things of the world of science that we have thought to be the truth, that they are not as they seemed. The beginnings of our world, the universe, the nature of matter, so many things that are too complicated for me to understand. What I do know, for certain, is that there is very little certainty."

"You are right. It is difficult for you to live that way."

The comment irked Francis. "It is more than just difficult. It undermines the basis of our living. I respectfully ask, has it ever occurred to you that our lives would not be so difficult if we only knew the answers to the questions that every one of us begs to have answered?"

"And these questions?" Jesus asked.

"There are so many, I hardly know where to start. But, I will start."

"Please do," Jesus said.

"We don't have any certainty if there is life after death. We just guess at it. I know that you have told us in the Bible that there is an afterlife where all will be good, that even our bodies will be whole again. But each one of us has to have a faith to believe that since you do not give us signs to know for sure. So, we just guess at it. I don't know about the others, but speaking for myself, I have to wonder why this is a secret.

"I want to know if my mother is there, my father, my dog Kiki. What about my sister who died in my mother's womb? Where is my brother Kenny? Is he a living person, or is he just dust in a box?"

The mixture of Francis's assertive talk and Jesus's

listening to what he already knew, yet perhaps never before heard spoken out loud, created a somber mood.

"There is more, if I may go on?"

Whether the look was a smile or a frown, Francis could not tell. *I might as well just go on,* he thought.

"Many of us want to know if the Father is a personal God. We want to know if he takes an interest in us. Or are there just too many of us for him to do that? We simply want to know.

"Do you know that there are some who think that God is indifferent to us, careless about us. When the children were being thrown into the fires, I have already asked you, where was the Father? Some wise men say that it all has a purpose, that some day in the next life we will be given an understanding about why.

Jesus held up his hand, as if signaling Francis to stop. "Francis," he asked, "do you believe in love?"

"Yes, I do. I know I'm not very good at it, but I believe in it."

"What do you mean by that?" Jesus countered.

"I don't know. I guess I believe that love is a good thing, that when a person has it that good things can happen to him. So, I believe that love is a good thing."

"And, Francis, when you have this good love, don't you give up a lot of yourself? I mean, doesn't it limit you, take away some of your freedom? I mean if you really have it, you can't just do whatever you want. It puts limits on you, obligations. Would you agree with that?"

"Yes, I would." And, still filled with guilt that he could not manage the responsibility of a wife and family, he said what he thought must be on Jesus's all-knowing mind. "And I know that I couldn't handle the obligations, the limits. I guess I'm just a loser."

Just in time to stop the gush of Francis's self-pity, Jesus said, "Faith is like love. It frees us and it limits us."

Whenever Francis was aware of his own short-comings, he grew bold, as if there was nothing to lose. "I don't know what you mean by that. It's just a lot of yadayada to me." As an afterthought, he said, "I'm sorry."

"What I mean is that faith gives a person a place to stand on, a place where he can feel that his soul is planted in good soil, nurturing soil. And, on the other hand, it keeps him from answering to the siren songs your Greek playwright speaks of."

"I guess," Francis murmured in a distracted way.

"Francis, I am a little surprised that you said before that the only guarantee Abraham and your customers had that everything would be okay is my word. I think that my word is really something special; not like the word of most people on earth, where it is as if you actually work at *not* keeping your word.

"Your politicians say one thing to get elected and do another later. Your fathers and mothers teach their children from early on to not expect them to keep their promises. 'We'll go for an ice cream after dinner,' they say, then when it's time they tell the child that they are too tired, maybe tomorrow. They make promises and forget, or are indifferent so many times that the child begins to learn not to trust anymore. It becomes part of the way they think about the word of others.

"You can be sure that my word will be honored," he said with a note of finality.

"I know this is what you say, Jesus, but how can we know? Do you see how many questions there are? It is as if I am speaking to a non-listening God. You say there is a heaven, that you count the hairs on our heads. But, and here is a big *but*, we never really know. And then when we think we might know, when there is the littlest sign that you might be answering us, speaking to us, we are not sure if it is just a need we have, or our imaginations at work. Always the imagination.

"We can get mixed up. We're told in the Old Testament that you can be a vengeful God, a fire and brimstone God. Then we're told later that the Father is a loving Father, the unconditional lover of everyone. Frankly, the switch in character, if I may call it that, leaves me feeling more confused. I don't know what to expect.

Francis rubbed the back of his neck and looked at the ceiling, breaking eye contact. It was hard to think and look into those fathomless eyes. "I hope you don't hate me, but you came to redeem us. We are a poor excuse for the finished product. We're still working at it. Please don't give up on us.

"I know that many of us do anything we can to have an easy life. We don't like suffering. But, please don't go by us here in America. We do not suffer much here. Go by those on the earth who suffer. See all of us in them. I'm afraid that most of us do not have the patience of Job. I wonder how many of us are like me, going to faith as a sort of backup, just in case you really do exist. We cover our bases. And that's no way to live. I think you want us to be free, to use our minds and wills to love, to do the right thing. Not act or say something because we are scared."

Francis was suddenly angry at it all. It was as if all the frustration in his whole life was bubbling up from he didn't know where. "Jesus, I am sorry, but I think about these things a lot. And I don't have any answers. When this happens, I just think more and harder. I am beginning to think that there aren't any answers. I mean, of course there are answers, but you choose not to let us know them. I am not so different from most others when I tell you how frustrated this makes us. We want to believe in you, but we are left guessing. Of course, because of this experience, I don't include myself in that anymore.

"I do not want to be disrespectful to you or to the Father, but you seem to want things your way here, even though we are free to choose differently."

"What do you mean by that?" Jesus asked him.

"You know what I mean, so why do you ask me?" Francis responded.

I hope I'm not going overboard with this, Francis thought. He realized that he was beginning to show anger and disrespect

"Let me ask you again, Francis. What do you mean by that?" Francis was beginning to realize the absurdity of his remark about God wanting to have it his way. Yet, he continued to press the point.

"Well, take Richard, for example. He wants to be the one who will get hit at the game, and you say no, that he's not quite himself, just starting to recover from his drinking. But he's not a drunk anymore. He knows what he is doing, and he's willing to be the sacrificial lamb here for us. It seems to me that you're taking away his desire, his free will."

"Not really, but you wouldn't understand."

"Here we go again," Francis blurted out. "I'm just so stupid. I'm just a really stupid human who couldn't understand what's going on even if you told me. Fact is, you just don't want to tell me."

And then he began to challenge Jesus. *This isn't like the story of the garden of Eden, when Adam was told to not eat the apple.* Jesus did not tell him to not ask questions, even if they seemed tinged with anger. "Isn't it true that you don't want us to know?"

"Yes, it is. But only because right now the information might seem very contradictory to you and to others. Francis, you seem to be angry. Why is it that you're so angry? You have been given the gift of life. It is a gift. Nowhere did the Father say that you would understand it. So, why are you so angry? It's all right to tell me."

"Oh, Jesus," Francis responded in a softer, more conciliatory tone. "I just don't get it. I don't understand why some people get hurt and others don't. You seem to be there for some and not for others."

"What do you mean? You imply that I play favorites."

"Well, that's because it appears that way, especially to those of us who are trying to believe. Just the other day I was reading in the paper about three teenagers who were hit head-on by a drunken driver. Two of the kids died. Do you know what the one who lived said?" Without waiting for an answer, Francis said, "'God was there for me. He didn't want me to die.' *He didn't want me to die.* Does that mean he wanted the other two to die? What kind of a God is that? It's a God who plays favorites, that's what it is.

"It's the same thing in war. One guy gets it and the other one next to him doesn't. The guy who doesn't says, 'God didn't want me to die.' Okay, good for him. But what about the other guy?" He stopped, looked up at Jesus, and pleaded for an answer. "What about the other guy?" he repeated.

When he said this, Jesus felt a great sadness come over him, a sadness born out of his last days on earth thousands of years ago. It was as if Francis was pressing the crown of thorns into his head again. He shivered.

"Do you see what you are doing, asking me these questions? You have this sense of me and the Father, that we are watching over and dictating every action that is done on the earth. Just because someone attributes their safety to God does not mean that God holds back the laws of science and nature."

"I understand that. I really do. What I don't understand is the purpose of living this life. You take the young soldier who is killed. A bullet strikes him in the head, and suddenly he's dead. He was born into a loving family, went to school, had friends, maybe a girlfriend he loved, and bam, he's dead. Just like that, he's dead.

"I just don't get it. What's it all about? If you had created a just universe, something like that, things like the stupidity of war where young people kill each other to make a point, would not happen." For emphasis, he repeated, "It just would not happen."

Francis was agitated. But he would have his say. "There was a young woman who once lived in Astoria here. I read about this in the paper. She was bright, went to medical school, got her degree. Her family who lived on Long Island had a backyard celebration in her honor. She was stung by a bee at the party and died.

"Now, that's just crazy. I don't mean that you or the Father are crazy. I mean that it happened is crazy. I didn't even know her, yet I think about her all the time. She was twenty-five years old. Think about it."

Jesus found it amusing that Francis wanted him to think about it, as if he hadn't already. He pretended to cough so that he didn't show how funny he found the remark.

"I mean if she had gotten to the party a minute earlier, a second later, the bee would not have been at that precise spot to sting her. If she had just skipped the mustard where the bee was, or if someone had said 'Hi,' and she moved to say 'Hi' back. Or a swat of her hand shooed the bee away. Do you see, if any one of a hundred things had happened differently, that young woman would be here today?

"She would be treating her patients, doing good things for the world. If I remember right, she wasn't married. But she might have had a boyfriend she loved. She might have told him one day that she loved him hard as starlight. And cried as he held her tight and wiped away the tears. She would have known a moment of pure love. For just a brief second she might have felt like you do all the time as you love each of us.

"I'm saying that I don't understand why she is dead, dead from the sting of a tiny insect. I just don't get it."

Jesus looked at Francis with a benevolence he had never known, not even from his mother. "I see. I see, too, how hurt you are, how you struggle with these questions. How sad and angry you are that there aren't any certain answers." The mailman accepted the offer of kindness, as he realized he was in the presence of a great compassion, a goodness beyond understanding. The moment of grace startled Francis, who began to feel a small opening of understanding, one that enabled him to know peace and an end to his questions, at least for the second.

"Jesus, please let me know if it's all right for them to go to the game."

"Tell them it's all right. But tell them, also, that the Father does not place limits on the laws that govern slap shots at hockey games."

30

Madison Square Garden on a Thursday night hockey game late in a hard-fought season is a special place, especially when the Rangers are the ones fighting for the last playoff spot.

In the big scheme of things, it is just a game. But who there on that night thought much about the big scheme of things? The crowds exiting trains, cars, and cabs to get to their seats on time are oblivious to all other drama except the need for a Rangers' win. This is not a team of baseball dandies who make the big bucks and go their own way after the games. Nor is it one man battling another. No, this is not a tennis match or a game of golf. This is hockey, the ultimate team sport, a game that is not unlike a jazz session, where each player must know the moves of every other player in the band. If they do not play off each other, their sounds become excuses for noise.

The ones who understand that hockey is being sucker-punched with a slam crunch to the body are truly fanatics. They know that hockey is drinking with the guys after the game. It is trying so hard that you'd rather die than not come back on the ice with twenty stitches in your mouth.

These are the guys who know blue-collar, guys you can root for. No pretty boys here.

"I forgot to tell them the part about the Father not interfering with the laws."

He had gone to each of the apartments to tell Tina, Richard, Bill, Cora, and Nicholas that it would be okay to take the kids to the game. When he remembered the part that there would be no special considerations, he called Ellen with an excuse to not meet up with Thomas and Kyle. He would go by himself, maybe give away the extra ticket or, better, sell it.

"You not only don't have faith in me, Francis. You don't trust me," Jesus said.

"What do you mean," Francis asked, trying to sound innocent.

"Do you forget that I know your every thought?" Jesus asked.

"But, I thought you are here as a man, Jesus the man."

"True, yet sometimes I tap into my Godhead. When I do that, I know what you are thinking. I do this only sometimes, and only with someone I know deserves this way of mine."

Francis was stunned at the implication. "How is it that I might deserve this from you? I have failed you."

"You have not failed me. You have worked hard for the mission to happen. Do not take responsibility for the others who have said no. Just be responsible for yourself. I know that you will not be bringing Thomas to the game, that you think I am leading you down the path to sadness, that Thomas might die at the game tonight. True, he might. Chances are, though, that he will not die, as being hit in the head by a puck that will break a blood vessel is most unusual. It is a small act of faith to go to the game, believing that you and Thomas will go home after it, alive and well. It is nothing more than you do hundreds of times each day ... walking down the street, getting on a bus, going to the movies. You do have some trust in the universe.

"I do not want to push you any further on the matter. Please know that it is a good thing not to take Thomas to the game. I admire your love for him."

Though it was not easy to shake off or forget that the Son of God had recently entered into their lives by way of the mailman or the foreboding talk about the hockey game, each of Francis's clients and Francis himself attended the game with their much-loved children. Francis had told them not to worry, and so they didn't. What most of them didn't think about is what they probably knew: that God, except in mysterious cases, does not interfere in the laws of the

universe. They just didn't know that Jesus had reiter-
ated that again. In a way, they went to the game as
innocents.

Being the most experienced of them all in the matter of death, Bill Waxman was on full alert as he and
Megan got to their seats. As soon as they sat down,
he sized up the positions of their seats as well as the
many angles that pucks, hard hit, might enter what
he thought of as their "free fire" zone. He was again
the Marine on Iwo Jima. He would build a foxhole
for Megan that might afford her the most protection
from the enemy.

"Megan, honey," he said, "switch seats with me."

"No, Grandpa, I like it here."

"Do as I say," and she did.

The roar of the crowd did not sound right to Bill.
There was something unusual about it. He was aware
that the game tonight was a critical one for Rangers'
fans. Most of the time, the crowd noises were a mixture
of the many kinds of fans in the crowd: the low roar
of the quiet, yet enthusiastic ones, who were probably
quiet in the days of their lives; the raucous ones who
played out their frustrations and participated by hard-
edged, manly yelling; the women whooping the signature yell of the liberated female. And then there was
the silence that was known only when it sounded off.

In all, it was a mixture with clear separations
and boundaries that could be discerned by a trained
listener. Tonight, though, was different. The crowd
noise sounded knit together to Bill, like the grunting
noises of leopards hunting their prey. He didn't want

to cheer in any way, afraid he too might become part of a pack of beasts slouching toward a kill.

There was fear in his stomach, the same kind he felt when he was on Iwo. He wasn't sure if he was just imagining things. Turning to Megan, he asked her if she was all right.

"Yes, Grandpa Bill, I'm fine. Everything is fine," she responded while cracking the popcorn he had bought for her.

Maybe I shouldn't have switched seats with Megan. Maybe I'm playing with fate. Although Francis had told him everything would be all right, his cynicism with God was active, especially this night. He would have to protect Megan against any possibility.

Sitting not too far from them was Cora Aldrich and Angelina. For Cora, the night at the Garden was a way to show Angelina how much she wanted to please her by filling her request, as well as marking another way to pull her daughter to herself and away from Bob, who probably was off seeking another woman whom he might impress for the night.

Angelina was especially excited as she watched the tall, muscular players for the Canadiens, also battling for a playoff berth, and the Rangers warm up. "Mom," she blurted out, "see how they glide. I like it the best when they seem like speedy sailboats moving together." She needed to explain. "I don't mean the ones going like the hands of a clock. I mean the ones going in the opposite direction. It's smoother, easier. The ones going like the hands on a clock seem to be pushing into the wind. They've got to try harder. I like the other ones," she repeated.

"That's a very bright observation," Cora said in her best reassuring and maternal way. If she couldn't find her way again after whoring around, she could, at least, help her daughter never to lose hers.

The months seeking *darklight* had not left her without a keen sense of the moment, an inner button that she could use to make watchful imagination and reality become one. When this happened, a green light flicked *on* for safe and a red one *off* for danger. Although she believed Francis that everything would be all right tonight, she found the red light blinking rapidly.

She sometimes used this intuition to look for signs from the not-speaking God. Any little trickle from the unknown, a shiver of wind that the curtain was being lifted a tad, was welcomed by her. She noticed that Angelina was bobbing her head first left, then right, to see over the tall man who was sitting directly in front of her. *A sign,* she thought.

"Angelina, why don't you switch seats with me so you can see better. It won't bother me to sit behind him," she whispered while pointing to the man in front. The switch was welcomed.

Meanwhile, with some difficulty, Nicholas was getting seated in the same section with Aaron. He was always glad to be with his son, though he was never sure of any reciprocal joy. He had spent a lifetime running from intimacy and tonight would be no different. At least, on the outside. In his heart, Nicholas longed to tell his son how much he meant to him, yet he did not have the skills to let go the prescriptions given to him early in life by his own father, who never let down his guard. He knew, too, that he could no longer pretend that he had forever in front of him. He knew that the remaining grains of his sand were running rapidly into the bottom half of the hourglass.

Nicholas noticed that there was one empty seat at the end of their row. "Aaron, why don't you sit at the end where you'll have a better view of the ice. It's a better place."

"But, Dad, what if someone has that seat?"

"Well, I guess, just move back and let them take it." As usual, Nicholas was not good at thinking about consequences. He moved one step at a time, seldom knowing where he was headed, or even where those he loved were going.

Tina tried a host of excuses to keep Christopher from going to the game, telling Joe that he had lots of homework, that he would not get a good night's sleep. Tina had actually made a dent into his continuing indifference to her, and he was actually giving her some room to be herself. He had even made a few overtures about getting the rabbit she wanted.

But when Francis told her that everything would be all right, she gave in.

"How do you like the seats, Chris?" Joe asked.

"I like them fine. Nice and close, a good place to watch the game." Given the random accidents that happen in life, this might not have been a "good place" to watch the game. Tina knew that there might not ever be such a place in life. Yet, she would go along with tonight. After all, didn't Jesus say that everything would be okay? Her mistake might have been, though, in taking the reassurance to mean that there was a special dispensation from the laws that govern man's actions that night.

Richard Darby was not yet capable of being fully aware of these considerations. The residue of his drinking, designed in part to keep him separated from awareness of weighty matters, had not yet evaporated from his system. It would take time. Ironically, in the most innocent way of being, he was swimming in the river of life, letting it take him wherever it might. He had offered himself to be the victim, to be in place of Erin, if that was what was needed. It could be a way back into her love, although he would never know it, at least in this life. That was all he could do. Nothing more, nothing less.

Without questioning, he took the computer-generated seats assigned to him and Erin by the ticket sales department. He thought the seats were all right, nothing special. He was more taken with a man two rows down from him who had just bought a large beer and took just one sip before placing it on the floor between his legs. Richard would have gulped it down before coming up for air. *How can anyone take such teeny sips?* he wondered.

Although he didn't order a beer, he couldn't resist trying to get a better seat for Erin. "Hey!" he shouted to one of the ushers.

"What can I do for you, sir?" he responded, eager to be of service. And rewarded, too, for his services.

"I was just wondering," Richard said, "if for a Hamilton my daughter and I might get a better seat?"

"It's a big night, you can see, but for a Jackson, I might be able to get you a front row. Only problem is, I might have to keep switching you if the seats get taken. You know, sometimes a customer shows late, busy at the office, or something like that. If that happens, I'll have to move you. Maybe even a couple of times, maybe even back here. Some nights it's like rolling the dice."

He was quick to add, "No refunds, though. I'm taking a chance here. I could lose my job. It's not allowed, what I'm about to do."

"Oh, Dad, could we? It would be so cool to sit down there," Erin said, pointing to a few empty seats directly behind one of the nets. Even though the twenty bucks would take its toll on his budget, Richard couldn't resist.

"Okay, let's give it a try," he said to the Jackson man.

The man leaned over and whispered, "Please slip me the money as part of a beer you can buy from that guy over there selling beer. He's my buddy and we have an understanding. He gets a buck from me. Just order the beer and say, 'This is for your bud,'" adding, "that's me."

To order a beer! The thing Richard probably most wanted in life. Even more than he wanted Erin to regard him with respect and affection. More than life itself.

He had been told at the meetings that there would be a moment like this. That if he could just hang on to what he had learned in the program, to think fast and sweep the bad alcohol experiences into the forefront of his brain as reminders of what this would do to him, this one beer. To remember that this one would lead to another, and to another. That there would never be enough. That by the third or fourth one, he would want to drink every beer from every vendor at the Garden tonight.

Spurred on by his growing love for his daughter, these reminders came to him quickly. He especially remembered the mangled body of his wife in the car that day. "Hey, buddy, I don't drink. You wouldn't happen to have a deal with the soda guy, would you?"

"Just slip me the twenty when I get you to your new seats. It'll look like a tip." Richard gave a quick *thank you* to his higher power, grabbed Erin's hand, and followed his benefactor, who placed them in seats directly to the right of the goalposts, behind the glass which was designed to stop frozen hard pucks that quivered through the night at over 120 miles an hour. *It is a good place,* he thought, *for Erin.*

Francis took the assigned seats, trying hard to guess about the one left empty by Kyle, suddenly sick that afternoon. The unoccupied seat gave Francis more to think about, another card to be played in the game of chance. Before he sat down, he asked Thomas which of the two he'd like. Without fanfare, he selected one. They both sat down, Thomas, Francis, the empty seat. Francis was delighted with himself, as he thought the simplicity of his actions might please Jesus, yet all the while calculating that by the law of averages, Thomas would be safe. But he knew, down deep, that he was still afraid.

Once the game began, Francis's customers, as well as the rest of the crowd, were taken up by the antics of rooting for the home team. A portion of the fans rooted because they needed to fill in the blank spaces within themselves by identifying with something bigger, in this case the Rangers. Others enjoyed the chance to simply yell their heads off, scream with gusto, something society would not allow them since childhood. It felt good to just blow out the pent-up frustrations of living in a big city, waiting for busses, rude bumpings, horns honking, hustling, speed, pedestrians staring, everyone into themselves, everyone scared of each other. Here was a place certified for noise and venting.

Actually, there wasn't much to root for. To the extent that fans were assertive, the reverse seemed true for both teams. They were holding back, each afraid to make the fatal mistake that might lose the game and position in the quest to gain a playoff berth. Eventually, both teams realized that this strategy did not work; that a speedier, more aggressive approach was needed. The skating became faster, less calculated. The body checking became fierce. Longer passes became the approach, each team hoping to get one of its streaky skaters on a breakaway to score the winning goal.

As this did not seem to work either, they took hard, distant slap shots, hoping to get a lucky bounce off a shoulder, a skate, a stick, and into the nets for the winning goal. It was then that it happened.

31

Before anyone knew what happened, Richard was sprawled under his seat, head down, feet sticking up onto his wooden seat, as if they were sitting there. Erin screamed when she saw the weird reconfiguration of her dad. It was as if he were shot by a sniper's bullet. He was screaming encouragement one second; upside down, bleeding, and unconscious the next.

A few asked Erin, "What happened?" Others directed, "Get him up on the seat." Still others, "Don't move him." Most of the fans had seen players hit in the head and knew how damaging a puck, ice-hard as a rock, could be to a person.

Erin knelt down and could immediately see that something was terribly wrong. The left temple of Richard's head had already swollen the size of half an orange. Blood was squirting from a tiny spot in the wound, as if there were some kind of mechanical force pumping it out in regular, short intervals.

"Someone get a doctor. Is there a doctor here?" the man to his left was yelling. Others began to wave a hand inward, beckoning someone, anyone, who knew what to do to come and do it. A mother sitting nearby took Erin close to her and asked her not to look at her father.

In time, Richard died, sitting in his seat next to the same man on his left who was trying to stop the bleeding by pressing his scarf against the flow of blood. Before the paramedics, doctors, and nurses could unfold their training to treat Richard, a blood vessel in his brain broke, ending his mostly tortured life.

When the pieces of the puzzle were put together, it was concluded that his story was ended by a puck that hit a metal pipe at the edge of the first section in the back of his seat. The shot was hard, and it deflected with enough energy to burst Richard's brain. The trauma doctor said later that it was like driving a nail into his head with a heavy, metal hammer.

It didn't take long for the others to see what had happened.

"Looks like Jesus got his way," Tina said. "He always does."

"I knew we shouldn't have come here tonight," an angry Nicholas yelled at Aaron. "Let's get out of here right now."

"Look at him. You'd think he was hit in the head by a sniper. I knew I shouldn't have trusted God. After all those years of not answering my prayers, why did I trust him now?" And then, without thinking, Bill said, "Thank God it wasn't Megan."

"I guess God got tired of poor Mr. Darby," Cora said to herself. "God the Father. I'm surprised he didn't work it out," she said sarcastically, "that a woman wasn't killed. Come on, Angelina, let's get home and call our wonderful mailman and see what he has to say about this."

The crowd seemed more excited about the interruption of the game than the game itself. It was a shocking experience for most, not used to being confronted with their mortality at a game where aliveness ruled. "Ladies and gentlemen," the public address system barked, "there will be a momentary delay in the game until order is restored. Normally, with an interruption of the sort we have just seen behind the Rangers' goal, we would consider postponing the rest of the game. However, as we are nearing the end of the season and tonight's game plays an important part in the standings, the game will resume, again, as soon as order is restored."

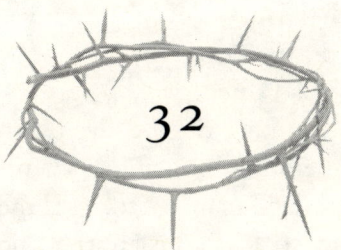

32

"Jesus," Francis said, "I guess you know what just happened to Richard Darby at the game?"

"Yes, of course."

They were again in their usual meeting place, Francis's living room.

"I've been getting phone calls from the group in the apartment. Some of them are really angry. They think that you tricked them, that you're angry at them for refusing your offer of faith, and that you went ahead anyway and had one of them killed."

Poor Francis. The guilt was mounting again. Did his forgetfulness, his failure to tell the group that there would not be any special protection from God for any of them at the game—was he the cause of Darby's death? After all, if he had remembered to tell them, perhaps Darby would have stayed home.

"I'm sorry. I didn't mean to mislead them. I just

forgot to let them know that things would be normal at the game, that you wouldn't provide any of them with any special protection."

Jesus seemed stunned.

"I have told you, we do not save one man in a fox-hole and have the other blown up. It happens that way because of where each man is sitting. If the human race could only learn to love one another, nobody would have to worry about where each soldier is sitting. I am sorry to say, Francis, that this is why the Father is growing weary with all of you. Joe is indifferent to Tina. Nicholas is self-centered. Cora is vengeful. Her Bob is, how do you say it? A basket case? Mr. Waxman needs to feel sorry for himself, wants special communications with God, something he does not even try to earn.

"And poor Mr. Darby. He never looked at his weakness face to face and confronted it, never had a desire to embrace his birthright as wonderful. His is the most ironic of all. Just when he was beginning to seize his ability to exercise his will, well, now he can't. The Father did not cause this to happen. Richard sat where he did."

Francis could hear the brisk, curt tone in Jesus's voice. He was scared, very scared. Yet at the same time he was beginning to know the role he was rapidly assuming: the mediator, not just between God and the selected families but, perhaps, between God and all of mankind. He was about to make things worse by blurting out a question that had nagged at him since forever. It was as if he had struck oil and couldn't stop the gush.

"Why did the Father make a world where animals eat each other? It is a horrible reality to me. I cannot give life. I cannot give life to even the smallest creature, an ant, a fish, even the tiniest bug so small that I can hardly see it. You give life. It is precious, sacred, mysterious. Yet, you have made it so that some of them eat the others. The baby chipmunk gets grabbed by the hawk."

Just as Jesus was about to respond, Francis cut him off. He didn't care anymore about being exact and polite. The certain instinct of self-preservation that mostly had automatically kicked in to monitor what he would say was no longer there. It was as if he simply did not care any more. The question about animals was the catalyst that turned spiritual frustration into indifference.

"I want to tell you a story," he said. Jesus pointed his chin forward slightly, and a Mona Lisa smile came across his face, as if he was amused that Francis might tell him a story. Or was the look one of annoyance?

"One day," Francis continued, "I was coming out of a big complex of fast food restaurants set alongside a superhighway. As I was leaving, I held the door for a well-dressed lady who had a tiny dog, a small peanut of a dog, on a leash. Just as they stepped out the door into the sunlight, a very large eagle grabbed the dog in its talons and swooped away into the sunlight, the dog's chain flapping in the wind. As the woman stood, surprised and horrified, her little dog let out a wailing sound that has never left me. No doubt, he was lunch for that eagle." He paused, then said, "I am bothered by things like that, very bothered. A beautiful dog, now a meal. I'll shut up in a minute, but I want to tell you that I am very bothered by people eating animals."

He had gotten it out, the worst thing, the thing that bothered him right to the foundations of whatever chance he might ever have to be a man of faith. And now he stood before the face of God, expecting an answer.

"Until Adam and Eve disobeyed, there was harmony on the earth. The animals, too, lived in peace with each other. With sin came disharmony, so even the animals became dysfunctional and greedy. Once some of them tasted other animal's blood, they no longer ate plants and vegetables. So it was, too, with man.

"You see, Francis, it is not a cruel world created by the Father. Whatever cruelty there is in the world has been created by man. But I must tell you that I am growing weary of it all. It hurts me in the spirit of my flesh to see the things that are happening here on earth. We have such wonderful dreams for you all. We have them in the eternal now. Yet, it became different in a way that I am sorry you cannot understand. You were to be an expression of my Father's love. He is love, you know. He wants to share who he is with everyone.

"Keep in mind, he does not have to do that. He wants to do that. It is his nature. And now ... I don't know what to tell you. I know that it is not sitting well with the Father. He is having another meeting with the Heavenly Council, and then will make a decision."

When Francis heard these words, an electric shock of anxiety coursed through his body.

"What do you mean that a decision will be made? What kind of decision? Please tell me."

"I am sorry, Francis, but the apocalypse might be upon you," the Son of God answered.

33

"Thank you, my dear friends, for being here with me again in this special way. I have grave news for you, and I am going to burden you beyond what you might welcome."

Albert, Juan, Arland, Dag, Diana, and Jimmy sat in wooden chairs next to Jesus, who, of course, was sitting at the right hand of the Father.

"Would you kindly curve your chairs around so we can face each other." And then, almost as an after-thought, "And you, too, my son."

"Before we start, I would like to say goodbye to Arland. Of course, it is not goodbye, really. It is what my Jewish people say *Shalom*. For me and Arland, it is not a goodbye to this Heavenly Council. It is an eternal hello."

Could it be that since the Father's Son had become flesh that he, too, being one with his Son, could also assume human ways? It appeared that when he said these words to Arland that there was a glistening in his eyes. Certainly, the soul of Jesus was touched by his Father's words. The magnificence of heavenly praise was still beyond Arland's comprehension. Someday, when he had achieved the fullness of his capacity to love he would understand what had just happened in the simplest of ways.

"Please, Arland," the Father said, "stay for the meeting."

"Thank you, our Father. I am humbled to be in your presence. I am beyond gratitude that I have been chosen as a member of the Heavenly Council, as I know I do not deserve the honor. Perhaps one day I will be able to give a name to the experience and the feelings it has engendered in me. They are new to me and right now they are indescribable." Always a clear and straightforward man, he simply bowed toward God and said, "Thank you, my Father."

"Let us resume our discussion," the Father said. "As has been evident for some time, I have become deeply disappointed in mankind on the planet Earth. When I first thought of him ... " He stopped, as if in reflection, before saying, "It wasn't as if I had a thought of him a first time. He has from eternity been in me, in what you like to call my mind. Anyway, when I created him, I had hopes that he would evolve like the creatures who are on some of the other planets I have created.

"In the end, man has been a failure. The ways are evident. So I have been contemplating ending his existence. Lately, in fact, I have been thinking about how this could be done without bringing pain, especially to the children.

"I could let them do it themselves by no longer holding back my hand. The ones who love on the earth ask me daily to keep the gates of hell from opening by atomic weaponry.

"I could allow the forces of nature to do it. Rising sea levels, simultaneous volcanic eruptions, a giant asteroid hit. Perhaps a genetic disease that would prevent gestation."

A collective gasp came from the members of the Heavenly Council. A nightmare in heaven? The extreme of childish fears once again? Thoughts beyond terror?

It seemed inconceivable for Jimmy Blackmore to hear what he was hearing. Ever since the evening when he died, he thought of little else than being together again with his wife and children, his loved ones. He did not want to think of them as dying in any of the ways iterated by the Father.

"You know how important you each are to me," the Father continued. "You are what I envisioned. And, sadly, you are unique. Do you see, because I am who I am, I know humanity in all the ways that he can be ... I mean your fellow man ... if only he would say yes to the gifts offered. His awareness, his consciousness, has the potential to soar with the angels here in heaven. If only he would say yes.

"I am extremely sad," he said, "in ways that you cannot understand. I know that people on earth think that because I am God that I cannot experience sadness. Through my Son, I can."

Like a jolting noise in the quiet, a voice rang out. "But, God the Father, you cannot do any of those things to my fellow man on earth, to my dear wife, to my children."

It was Jimmy Blackmore.

"Mr. Blackmore," the Father said, "my son has told me that you are a man of great passion. I like that in a man. Please continue."

If faces had color in heaven, Jimmy's would have been red. "I am so sorry that I blurted it out like that. Please forgive me," he said.

"There is no need for forgiveness, my son. No need at all. Please continue."

"I only know," Jimmy said, "that my loved ones on earth do not deserve what you speak of. I know there are some bad people. But most people are not that way. I know we have character weaknesses, but most of us are not bad. You would catch up all the good ones with the bad." He stopped for a minute and seemed embarrassed that he was out front so fast with God and the committee.

"Father," he said, "I have a better idea." But, the enormity of what he had just said was upon him. "I think it a better idea for me to sit down."

"Stay standing and say your mind. It is why you are here," interrupted Jesus, as if directing him.

"What I want to say is this. Father, if you are not happy with the way humans are working out their destiny, you do not have to destroy them. They will do it themselves. Perhaps, too, when they realize what they are doing, they will make attempts to stop. Once they realize the damage they do to each other, to the things around them."

Filled with the love of his family, Jimmy continued in the same way he dashed into the fiery building to save the woman he thought was there. "Jesus, may I speak directly to you?"

"Of course. Please."

"I know that you don't need reminding, yet I want to ask you to look again at why you came to earth." Calling on the love and respect that Jesus had for members of the group in front of him, Jimmy continued. "None of us here on the committee really know why you assumed our flesh and came to earth. I mean, we know that you came to redeem us, but you never said how angry you might have been with us then. We know from the stories that you could get angry and did get angry, but the kind of wrath you are speaking about here today is way beyond that. It is not simply getting annoyed at moneychangers or those who might misunderstand you. We're talking here about an angry cloud of darkness coming over the world.

"I beg you, in the name of all the good people of the earth, to let the darkness come from man himself, if it will. From you and the Father, it is beyond darkness. It will be not just taking away the light. It will be a horror beyond imagination. Please do not take away the light.

"Jesus, God the Father," he repeated, "please do not take away the light." Jimmy began to weep. He did this sometimes when he would think of his wife. And then he said, "May I please say one more thing?"

The Father and Jesus simultaneously answered, "When thou wilt."

And then Jesus did something the others had never seen him do. He went to Jimmy, looked him in the face before grasping his shoulders, one with each hand. "You are indeed a good man, James Blackmore. I love you and will never leave you. Nor your loved ones. Be certain of that." He then kissed Jimmy on his forehead in a way so gentle as to be unspeakable.

If it were not that Jimmy had already been in heaven for ten years and knew some of its ways, he might have fainted.

"What I wanted to talk about is the light. And my wife. Whenever I think of her I think of light. When I was on earth, in love with her, when I couldn't get her out of my mind, I would always think of her as taking up a little spot on the earth, maybe just a few feet around. And light would come from her, as if she had thousand-watt amorphous light filaments under her skin, wrapped around her but under her skin. I figured it wasn't real, that I just imagined it.

"Yet, it didn't make any difference that maybe I was making it up. It was real, very real, to me. At moments like that, I didn't care about anything else because when I was with her I knew that I was loved, that she loved me.

"You know, I never really felt worthy to be loved by someone like her. But when I would tell her this, she would have none of it. She would just give me the look, the one that said how silly I was being to think I was not worthy. Do you know, Jesus, there was something of you and the Father in her. What I mean is that I always felt that she loved me absolutely and without any reservations.

"I just wanted to let you know that when I thought about her or was in her presence that I didn't care about anything else. As long as I was in the light she gave off, well, then I was perfectly happy. When I was with her, there was nothing missing.

"I think that many others on earth are the same way. It is how they see those they love. Who am I to say what I will say? I know I have been given the gift of life, and now I am in heaven. I am grateful beyond words or my spirit to express it. I say this to you, knowing that I am speaking with my God. And so what I want to say is more like a request to you, a humble request." Jimmy shivered. Such was the moment.

"I can see that you are angry at the world. I just want to remind you, if I may, that when you came to redeem the world, Jesus, that it was by the will of the Father, it was in answer to the gift he offered to you. A most difficult gift. You were asked if you would share in the love of the Father for all of mankind, weak as we were. You were asked if you would suffer on the cross. I mean, really suffer. I do not believe it was any make-believe thing that you did. You know, only pretending that you were a man. That when things began to happen, when you were betrayed, whipped, crowned with thorns, nailed to a cross, watched your mother cry, that these could have been just make-believe. You could have faked it. I believe, though, that the suffering was very real. The kiss from Judas...if he had stabbed you through the heart it would have hurt less. The thorns in your head, worse than long, thin nails struck by a hammer. Your feet and hands nailed to wood. I shudder at the thought. I have never been whipped, but I can imagine.

"The hard part for me is that these things were being done to the Son of God, the Son of God. Can you imagine?" he asked without thinking of who was listening.

Such was his love for Jesus that Jimmy fell on his knees and began to cry again. He had never before wept like this. If he didn't stop right now, he thought that he might cry forever into eternity. He would not like Sue to see him that way.

"Please, my son, stand up. You have in the spirit known the wonder of the Father and me. As time goes by, you will know it ever more. So much more that your tears today will fade into a joy that right now you cannot even imagine. And be certain that your loved ones will be united with you in a happiness and in a peace beyond understanding."

Jimmy stood up, gathered himself, and continued. "The hardest part must have been to see your mother cry that day. It is a most difficult thing for a mother to see her son die before it is her own time. I know, as I have seen this happen to my mother who loved me much.

"Please remember that you once came to save us. We were poor, wretched creatures then, even as we are now. We were full of faults, even as we are now. We tried and failed, again and again. Our weak side surfaces over and over. You loved us then. I think you do not love us less this day. Please remember the good people, like my son and daughters, my Sue. Do not abandon us now. Do not cease to believe in us.

"Please, I beg you, give us another chance."

The members of the Heavenly Committee each came over to Jimmy and hugged him. Arland walked to Jesus and said, "He speaks for all of us."

One last thing remained. Jesus asked Francis to gather everyone together so he could talk with them all before saying goodbye. "I assure you, Francis, they will not be afraid. I'm sorry to disappoint you, but they won't even need a little miracle," he chuckled.

34

"Thank you all for coming here to Francis's apartment. I am indebted to him for all the work he has done in recent days. We have walked the road together, a long and difficult walk. I want now to speak with you all as a group. I think you are ready.

"I came here to earth two thousand years ago because the Father asked me to come, to do his will for the human race. He wanted to redeem mankind and the sinfulness that came after the Fall. We were, in the ways that are not understandable to you right now, optimistic that you would accept his love.

"Because you have failed, I have come again in the name of the Father. Again, you are failing the vision we have for you. So, we have talked. We have not ever pre-ordained what will happen, because you have been given free will. It is not contradictory to you, though, to tell you that we know what will happen. We always know. It is just that right now you do not know how to handle contradictions. You deal so much from your mind and not enough from your heart, which will tell you things you do not know with your minds.

"The Heavenly Council has been helpful. They are, if you do not know, a part of a Mystical Body. They are your advocates. We have listened to them because they have lived on earth and they know how difficult it is to be a good person, to say yes to the gifts offered by the Father.

"The four of you and Francis have made it no less difficult by saying no to the gift offered from the Father through me. Again, though, I am grateful to Francis.

"The Father has decided to give you another chance." They thought he was referring to their unwillingness to offer their loved ones, as opposed to Abraham offering Isaac. Jesus kept from them the Father's talk with the Heavenly Council.

A palpable buzz of happiness ran through the room. Francis, who had taken much of the burden of failure upon himself, looked especially relieved. It was a reprieve from the dark scourge of the Old Testament that could have overcome the earth. Jesus was also in his joy, at one with his love of the Father's will, his love for these creatures made in the image of the Father.

"We have a request to make of each of you," he continued. "We want you to know that we love you here where you live, in ways that are hard for you to understand. You are especially dear to us, though we do not love others less. Another contradiction, I am afraid, you will have to live with for now.

"The Father and I would like each of you to straighten out your lives, reveal your loving selves, especially to your families. We would like you to say yes to every inclination you have to honor, love, and respect each other. By that I mean every person, animal, plant, or tree that comes into the path you walk. We mean *every* person, animal, plant, or tree. No exceptions."

They didn't know why, yet each of them felt the word *every* as if it were accentuated, not just as a word in their minds, but as a word that lived in their hearts in a way that was different from the usual decoding. Sound, interpretation, meaning—all came together in a vortex of mind, heart, and soul. They knew exactly what Jesus meant.

"We would like to rely on you, so that if we ever in the near future are deeply disappointed once again, we can look to you. Will you do this for the Father?" he asked in a solemn sort of way.

Each of the four, followed by Francis, assented, then bowed low.

Cora Aldrich walked over to Francis, and reached out her hand to him. "Please give this letter from us to Jesus and to the Father. From us, please. It is right for you to be the one. We wrote the letter together last night."

He took the letter and handed it to Jesus. "Thank you, each of you," Jesus said, "I will bring the letter to the Father, as you ask. I want to tell you how I love you. It is like a gift from my Father, yet not really. I too am of the essence of the Father. One day you will know how this can be. Let it just be said that we love you beyond the love of a mother for her newborn baby, for that love is but as a drop in the oceans of our love for you.

"We want you to live in harmony. We want you to accept the laws of nature. We want you to know that things happen according to these natural laws and human ways. You cannot change natural laws. You can, though, change your ways. Say yes and believe that goodness will prevail." He hugged each one and looked deeply into each of their eyes before whispering something personal, one at a time.

"I am leaving you now," he said. "You will remember nothing about what has happened in the past few days. We have decided to do this for you so that you will not be burdened. You will only remember as an impulse your promise to say yes.

"Goodbye, my dear friends," he said softly, "Goodbye."

EPILOGUE

Dear Jesus, Dear Father,

It's us. Tina, Bill, Cora, and Nicholas. We wish that Richard was here. We trust he is with you today. And, oh yes, Francis is here.

We are all sorry that we have disappointed you. We are beginning to understand, just a little, that we can trust you. We have seen your loving ways. Please keep in mind (we know this is a funny way to talk with you) that we are weak people. Please remember the times when you might have felt that way, the temptations you must have had. We know that you overcame them. And we know that you are God. We are not.

We do know, though, that we are made in your image. We will try very hard. We want to ask you to remember the night before you died when you asked the Father to take away from you the burden to satisfy his love for us. It can be very hard to do the right thing. Sometimes, we wish we didn't have to.

We promise to try harder. In your image, we say back to you (Tina helped us with this), "Abba, Father, all things are possible to you. Remove this cup from us. Yet not what we will, but what you will."

We will never forget you. We will never forget your letters.

With love and respect, we remain,

Nicholas, Tina, Bill, Cora,
and Francis the Mailman